HARVEST TIME

DAN FIELDS, CHRIS ROBINSON, AND JOE FILIPAS

Crystal Lake Entertainment
www.CrystalLakePub.com

"Fields, Robinson, and Filipas will drive you deep into the heartland of terror in *Harvest Time*, a nightmarish roadtrip through a drought-stricken Nebraska where the land is barren and the skies are empty of everything except for black crow wings. Gruesome, unflinching, and wryly funny, this book will forever change how you look at crows, remind you to get your tires and engine checked regularly, and maybe cross Nebraska off your vacation list. And beware: when your eyes are on the sky, it's the rustle down in the corn that will get you."

— Jonathan Louis Duckworth,
author of *Have You Seen the Moon Tonight?
and Other Rumors*

"*Harvest Time* reads like Alfred Hitchcock's *The Birds* smashcut with Stephen King's *Children of the Corn* and George Romero's *Night of the Living Dead*. If you find murders of crows and marauding agro-zombies terrifying—I do—then prepare yourself for a white-knuckle road trip into America's heartland of darkness. In *Harvest Time*, the unholy trinity of Fields, Robinson, and Filipas have devised a devilishly entertaining read."

— Robert Eversz,
author of *Shooting Elvis*

"*Harvest Time* by Dan Fields, Chris Robinson, and Joe Filipas is a creepy peek into the horror of the desolate, rural Midwest. It'll leave you with a healthy aversion to corn, crows, and more. I definitely recommend picking up a copy!"

— Shawna Borman, author and blogger

"If *Hee Haw* or *Green Acres* had been written by Thomas Ligotti while he was having a rough day, you'd get something like this book."

— Craig Kringle, producer and
host of the Weird Christmas podcast

To Bill Bleich
(Thank you for the matches)

PART ONE: THE GOOD OF THE LAND

(YESTERDAY)

CHAPTER ONE

Six Days on the Road

The man standing in the middle of the highway had the look of a lonesome filling station geek who stared at the sun for company. He was either quite old or just wrecked beyond his natural years. Under the brim of a straw hat with the crown worn through, his eyes were taut with what looked like fear. Above his head, the man flailed a pair of bony arms. If the knockdown shack just up the road turned out to be his home, his business, or both, his greatest fears ought to have been a grease fire and a good strong wind. Plagues of rats or locusts would not bother stopping in such a place.

JT, sitting behind the wheel of a seven-ton camper, briefly considered putting the hammer down. Let the human roadblock dodge for his life. But for all he knew, denizens of this particular Nebraska backwater were too crazy to get off the road out of harm's way. In their shoes, given the scenery and the general vibe of rural despair, he might have welcomed a chance to become roadkill.

Katy, his wife, had been dozing in the passenger seat. Now she sat up and pointed.

"JT, look!" she said, as if he hadn't already been looking. "We have to stop."

"Katy, for crying out loud," said JT. "We just got going again after that mess on the interstate."

"He's not thumbing on the shoulder, JT. He's on the center line."

"Well, I declare!" JT said. "So he is, Inspector."

Katy punched him on the shoulder. "He might need help," she said. "Let's just ask what he wants."

"Whatever he wants, we don't have a spare jug of," JT snapped. "Am I the only one who wants to sleep in Colorado?"

JT tensed as a hand fell on his shoulder from behind. His

brother Bobby, freshly roused from a nap in one of the rear bunks, had come forward to join the debate.

"Will all you dumbasses quit pawing me while I drive?" JT said.

"Plenty of daylight, brother," Bobby said in the same quiet tone their mother would have used. "That guy looks like he has real troubles."

JT remembered a phrase their mother had reserved for people in dire-looking circumstances: "More troubles than a run-over possum."

"Slow down," said Katy. "If you're going to drive past, you don't have to kill him."

Something about her emphasis of the word *going* nettled JT. He had started the day in reasonably good spirits, but his soul had coasted downhill in the quiet way it did sometimes without his noticing. Delays, minor mishaps and false jogs had filled their last two days of driving, and JT felt ready to kill if it would cut a few minutes off the remaining journey.

Bobby's girlfriend Lisa materialized from the rear cabin. She had napped for most of the previous eighteen hours, and her blonde mane corkscrewed in multiple directions. At least she was dressed, which made her a more modest and agreeable roommate than the frequently bare-assed Bobby.

"What's shaking, nerds?" she said through a yawn, then grabbed JT's armrest. "Whoa, JT!" she said. "Ease up on the gas. Don't splatter the locals."

Swallowing a nasty reply on his tongue, JT hissed out a sigh and applied the brake. There would be more battles to fight, and he resolved to stand his ground or die the next time his passengers gave him trouble.

He had nearly faced a mutiny after deciding to exit the interstate prematurely. Held up for nearly an hour by a septic truck stranded on four flats, he'd let the impatient rumble of the camper's idling engine get to him and made a rogue detour.

As Katy hollered her objections, and Bobby whooped it up with Lisa like a pair of roller coaster riders, JT had nosed the motorhome off the shoulder and across fifty yards of grass to the access road. He'd regretted the decision as soon as the front end dipped into the deceptively deep ruts across the grass, but he'd had to keep his foot down and ride out the crash dive like those poor bastards in *Das Boot.*

After the front wheels found purchase on the far shoulder, and JT eased into the passing lane behind a horse trailer, Bobby and Lisa had cheered. All Katy had wanted to know was how far the detour would take them off the main highway. This trip had taught them all about her anxious attachment to well-marked routes.

Bobby had tried to help with a long and futile study of the highway atlas, until JT's patience broke down.

"Bobby, you read a map like Mom does."

"And you drive like Dad."

Lisa had reached for the map then. "Bobby, let me,"

"Somebody please tell him where to turn," Katy had moaned. "We'll end up in Kansas. I don't want to go to Kansas."

Katy's book club had read *In Cold Blood* six months before, and it had colored her view of Kansas permanently. Dreams of senseless murder troubled her sleep several times a month. JT had decided if she ever pestered him about moving to California, he would give her a copy of *Helter Skelter* to read.

Lisa had made sense of the route in three seconds. "I don't know whether we're on 47 or 21, but it's the same turn either way, through Farnam."

That had brought a wicked grin to JT's face. "Look at that, bro. You found a girl with a sense of direction. Hang on to her in case you can't find your ass in the dark. Lisa, if he doesn't propose, you can be my second wife. You know, in a strictly administrative capacity."

"Gee whiz," Katy said. "What woman could say no?"

"Insubordination is grounds for replacement," JT shot back. He watched her with one eye until she cracked a grudging smile.

"Thanks, JT," said Lisa, still studying the map. "So glad I agreed to spend weeks locked in this lumbering fart-wagon with the three of you. You should see signs for the junction with 23 in a few miles. Turn right and follow it to the state line."

Everyone had gone quiet after that, but calm had settled in place of apprehensive silence. Making time felt good, and JT had smiled, thinking of the suckers left on the interstate. For the first time that day, they'd known where they were going.

Now this.

The old man in the road didn't look any happier as the camper pulled over, but his lips pulled outward across ash-colored gums as he trotted toward them. His loose-limbed gait suggested a hastily cobbled imitation of humanity.

Bobby moved toward the door as JT brought the vehicle to a stop. "I'll talk to him."

"Like hell," said JT. "You'll spend twenty minutes taking his picture. I'll talk to him."

When he swung the door open, JT was startled to find the man already there, hat in hand, practically leaning into the camper with the same waxy rictus on his face.

"What's the problem, man?" JT asked, his best attempt at being casually polite.

The stranger looked uncertain, threw a glance down the highway, then peered past JT to see who else was in the camper. JT wondered why he had come to the door without grabbing Bobby's old Louisville Slugger first, or at least the jack handle. Not that the guy was visibly much of a threat, but having something to brandish was a comfort.

"Look, we're trying to make time here," JT said. "What is

it you want?"

"I was, ah…" the man stammered. His poor mind appeared to be overheating. "I just wondered if you folks wanted to see inside." He stepped back, giving a feeble wave at his roadside hovel.

Nailed over the door was a tin sign with raised letters: NEBRASK EMPORIUM

JT could not decide whether the sign was misspelled, or had lost an "A" that the management could not afford to replace. In a dust-shaded window just below, a rumpled card proclaimed, "See Rare Treshures Of The Corn State!"

JT could not help laughing. "Seriously, that's your pitch? You ever consider building a bigger sign?"

Bobby shoved past them, beaming at what he must have taken for quaint splendor. His camera was out. The man stumbled back, raising a protective arm as if snapshots might blow the building over. Once he saw Bobby smiling, and the girls climbing out to have a look, he relaxed.

"This place is classic," said Bobby, kneeling to get a low angle against the cloudless sky. "You got, like, a two-headed chicken in there, or an Aztec mummy?"

The man heard the question, but comprehension did not register on his face. "We got some snakes," he said. "Some real good ice cream, also," as if the two went together perfectly. He slid a hand up his skinny forearm and scratched at an unsanitary-looking bandage. JT could see a rim of red where the wound had seeped, probably from not being left alone to heal.

Bobby looked oblivious to bad omens, clutching the camera he'd spent most of the trip fiddling with. JT had been surprised to learn it was a digital SLR, identical to the old 35-millimeter Canon he'd always toted around, but with all manner of extra dials and a large viewfinder screen on the back.

He detached a long-range lens, unwieldy as a can of

hairspray, with which he'd snapped a handful of scenic vistas during food and fuel stops, as well as numerous gnarly road accidents from the passenger-side window. The big lens went into a padded pouch he wore on a strap over one shoulder, and Bobby replaced it with a standard-sized one.

"I brought macro filters too," he said, mostly to himself. "In case they've got weird miniatures and shit inside."

"Fascinating," said JT. "I hope all your shots of highway carnage left space in that thing for cornfield oddities."

Katy made a face.

Bobby laughed. "Not a problem! I went through everything last night. Sorted all my keepers into folders by date, location, and theme. Freed up a ton of memory."

JT shook his head. "I never thought you'd go digital."

"I know, I know, Mister Purist. At a certain level of use, it's just practical to have immediate access and full editing capability. Besides, these things are built with all the manual controls for when you want them. It can do everything the old-fashioned way, plus ten times more."

"Sorry," JT said. "That's just no consolation to folks like me."

It was a well-weathered debate between them. JT was glad Bobby had a creative outlet, but despite his natural eye for composition, he was too damned pragmatic for art. Bobby's standard reply was to call JT a contrarian and a dinosaur, too paranoid to embrace the digital age. JT did not consider this a criticism and could never explain to his brother the perverse pleasure he took in those photos on every roll of film that, for one reason or another, came out wrong. Only after a long and stubborn argument had he persuaded the others to stow their personal phones in a locked safety box near the back of the camper, to be retrieved only at the end of the trip or in a genuine case of life and death.

"Hurry up and get your gruesome snaps for posterity," JT

said. "We're not staying long."

Bobby grunted. "Easy, bro. You don't find photo ops like this every day. Anyway, Lisa's dragging ass today and I'm dying to get a shot of her in front of this place." He flinched, almost dropping his equipment in the dirt as a small fist punched him in the spine.

"Who's dragging ass?" Lisa said.

She and Katy posed for Bobby's camera in front of the "Treshures" sign. JT watched them while the old man watched JT. Katy sported cutoffs and one of JT's button-up fishing shirts, while Lisa had the P. J. Soles look in her overalls and an outrageously pink pair of Chuck Taylors. He wondered if they knew or even cared how much they looked like the city kids who spend the first hour of a horror movie getting high and teasing the locals. Cue the arrival of psychos in skin-masks wielding power tools, and the next carload of tourists could purchase ice cream with bits of JT and company mixed in.

"Come on, man," said Bobby. "You only go around once."

JT considered turning the phrase around to argue that they should make the most of their day and get the ever-loving hell out of this dry hole. Instead, seeing that he could not corral them voluntarily back to the camper, he stepped out and slammed the door.

"Fine," he said to nobody as the others ran inside. "But we're not making one more stop for root beer floats, pregnant hitchhikers, or the Second Coming." He clung to the reassuring notion that sneaking up on people with an idling chainsaw must be impossible in real life.

The Emporium had been a filling station in a past age. Hay bales were stacked high on the cracked and pitted concrete apron out front, ancient pumps all but hidden from view behind them. A Sinclair Oil sign, its green dinosaur shot full of holes and nearly faded away, hung next to the front door. The prices indicated that the place had not serviced motor vehicles for most of a generation. The convenience store layout had been kept intact, but instead of six-packs and tire gauges the shelves were lined with curiosities and unsold trinkets fashioned by unskilled hands. Hammered metal placards for corn festivals, corn products, and the general virtues of corn were the chosen decor for every available square inch. For a building with four standing walls, the place had an impressive layer of grit blanketing its interior surfaces. The cool, mellow darkness maintained by the filthy windows was a blessing. Otherwise they might have baked alive.

Katy edged aside to let the others explore, keeping both hands at her sides as if afraid of touching anything. JT watched with a trace of sour amusement as she backed into a corner where a silent figure crouched. She yelped as a gloved finger poked against her shorts.

Turning, she faced a portly scarecrow seated on an antique diesel can, spreading its arms in welcome. Dry corn-husk innards bulged between the buttons of its threadbare denim shirt. A gas mask from some bygone war effort sat atop the shoulders where a head ought to be.

"Go on," said Lisa, "sit in his lap. Bobby, get a picture!"

"Won't hurt you none, ma'am," said the owner. "He's just for funnin'."

Katy would not sit.

The only light came from the ice cream case, a glass coffin showing a fresco of greasy fingerprints. The motor rattled and bucked as if it ran on a two-stroke mixture. Inside, two tubs of half-melted matter the color of smoker's teeth sat ready for their enjoyment. Pasted along the top panel was a strip of paper announcing, "Finest Nebraska Hand-Dipped Ice Cream."

They had snakes too, as promised. Next to the ice cream chest was an identical model stripped for parts and converted to a crude terrarium. Instead of a live python, which it seemed big enough to hold, someone had arranged the skeletons of a dozen baby snakes in a tiny parade. Their bristly bones, cleaned of skin and muscle by God knew what primitive process, were the most intact artifacts in the whole store. As Bobby snapped away with his camera, the owner blundered in his direction, trying and failing to seem chummy.

"Say, friend. Wonder if you fellers would be interested to try some of that real Nebraskan ice cream. They don't make nothin' else like it in the nation."

"Oh, I don't know," said JT. "I saw a TV film once where they fed stuff like that to chickens and veal calves."

The old man shot JT a look, as if he'd just picked up on the young stranger's attitude and would like to shut his mouth. Then his eyes darted to the far wall. JT sensed that something else weighed on the man's mind, something he did not want to say.

"Just thought you might, is all," he said quietly. "I'm worried about my freezer. It's a wonder it ain't give out already. Be an awful waste."

Bobby piped up, looking impish. "Hey, if it's cold and sweet, we'll take four."

JT dealt his brother a narrow-eyed grimace. "Sorry, Bobby. Not on a Friday. It's against our religion, remember?"

Bobby offered his most charming screw-you smile in return. "Hell, JT, we can backslide a little, can't we?"

The old man looked from one to the other, a dim awareness of their mockery in his eyes. He shuffled toward a stack of Dixie cups on the windowsill above the freezer. He had a tarnished soup ladle for a scoop. JT had thought "Hand-Dipped" might mean he served it with his fingers. Four equal portions of the golden glop were handed around.

"A buck a throw please, sir. Mighty steep, I know, but I can't charge two bits for no ice creamy treat anymore. Hard times."

Bobby handed over five bucks with a dignified look of pity. When he made no sign of wanting change, the man nodded.

"I thank you, friend. I do."

Katy's limited enthusiasm was long gone. Lisa, all nervous giggles, grabbed her to look at a moth-eaten display of amateur taxidermy. The presiding theme was "still life with corn." One notable piece was a fat red fox squirrel, apparently captured when the proprietor had visited some faraway place with actual trees. Its bushy tail had fallen out in patches, and its scrawny paws were stapled around a withered cob in a sort of bear hug. The thing stood on a short plank of knotty pine, across which a child's wood-burning craft tool had been used to write "Gone Too Nebraska."

"Come on," said Lisa, "how often do we get to see something this weird?"

"Every time we get together, it seems like," Katy said without much humor.

Bobby took a hard swallow of his ice cream, picking a wisp of cornsilk from the corner of his lip. JT gave his cup a sniff and set it down on a shelf.

"I'll be outside," he said.

The old man watched JT go, then watched his ice cream sweat down the side of the cup. "You... You folks gonna stay around for the harvest fair?"

There had been a fairground maybe thirty miles back, with several animal pens mostly rotted apart and a striped canvas pavilion, partly burned. There were no banners, or any live crops in the surrounding countryside, to indicate a harvest worth celebrating in the past few years. How long ago had this character last seen a newspaper or been into town? Never mind how he lived from day to day.

Bobby shook his head. "I, uh… We're just passing through."

"We'll catch it on the way back," Lisa said with a grin.

The old man nodded, evidently judging this a sensible plan. He scratched absently at his hurt arm again. "Most folks just pass on through. Harvest fair ain't much like it used to be anyway—not like when I was a boy."

"Big drought, huh?" Bobby said. "Nothing to harvest."

"Things is changing," was all the old man said. He studied the ground again, avoiding something he clearly wanted to say. He would probably ask them to stay for dinner.

Outside, JT slid a smashed pack of smokes from his hip pocket and shook out a dented Marlboro, one of the few he had left. Katy had been working on him for a year to taper off and finally quit, but the desolation around him made a double lungful of sweet poison seem like the dearest thing in the world.

Katy did not object to his finishing whatever smokes he had on him—outside the RV and away from camp, if possible— and he had pledged not to buy another pack until they were on the way home. His lighter, as much a sentimental reason to keep up the habit as any, was engraved with a round "No Smoking" logo and the words "LIFE'LL KILL YA," which was partly a nod to the Warren Zevon record, partly a private joke with an old band mate who would eventually fall asleep at the wheel, running a beautifully restored Chevelle into an oak tree four times his age. Hell of a bass player. At least cancer never got him.

Shielding his flame from the breeze, JT peered up the road

toward the Colorado paradise that slipped away with every minute of the afternoon. A lone figure shambled up the far shoulder, a younger man than the owner of the corn stand but no less leathery and disheveled. His bald head was the only clean pink part of him. He swung a brown bottle in one fist, jabbering as he moved along the verge of another dead cornfield. High above, a trio of vultures circled an unknown meal hidden in the rows.

JT kept still, watching the newcomer rather than attract his attention by moving away. He wished he had Bobby's camera. The bleak picture of man, crops, and scavenger birds captured the sinking melancholy that had pulled at him all along this leg of the drive. He had been expecting to see America, but the route they had chosen had been like seeing the underside of a log kicked over, moldy black and crawling with termites. He prayed Colorado would be green, with water swirling around the great rocks and enough crisp air to banish his blues. If they could only get there.

The drunk took notice of the great black birds above him, sheltering his eyes as a sickening leer cracked his face. "Not today, you bustards!" he croaked with glee. Not buzzards or bastards but bustards. "I knows myself better."

The man pointed two fingers like a pistol and mimed shooting them down. They soared placidly on as he spat bullet sounds through flapping lips. Clouds of spittle issued forth until his breath grew ragged.

JT was about to turn away when the gaunt body swiveled. They locked eyes, and the drunk fired an imaginary shot through JT's forehead. "Not all so lucky, sometimes."

JT was pretty sure that was what the guy had muttered. JT shot him the finger, the regular one. The drunk seemed to enjoy this, cackling as he turned the gun hand on himself with an approving nod, and fired.

Rather than see if his new friend would come over to chat,

JT walked away determined to get the party moving. Something foul grazed his heart. He could sense the wino's eyes on him. The doorway to the store was blocked by the slant of the owner's back. Bobby was arguing with him, trying to get past.

CHAPTER TWO

Man's Best Friend

Growing up, JT used to joke with Bobby that the state of Nebraska did not exist. It had started with an ordinary after-dinner conversation—ordinary for their family. Bobby asked a question about his geography homework, JT made up some lie to tease him, and then they argued about it until Mom told them to ask Dad. Instead, they kept arguing. The only thing JT remembered clearly was how the conversation ended. Dad, who bitched about noise and watched every football game with the sound muted, had growled at them from his fraying corduroy recliner.

"Nebraska? Son, that's in the god-blamed middle of nowhere! How the hell should we know when it became a state? Who cares if it ever did? Now both of you shut up." Dad was a self-made man and no dummy, but he frequently missed the point of higher education.

From that day on, both boys pictured a hole in the universe with the familiar chipped rectangle shape of the so-called Cornhusker State. Nothing they ever learned about the place, including its nickname, convinced them of its reality. By the age of thirty, JT had met only two people claiming to come from Nebraska, both times in social situations where his relentless question, "No, where are you from really?" fell flat into awkward silence. He had never met a Nebraskan with a sense of humor; of that he was certain.

He and Bobby had tried at various times to explain the Nebraska thing to friends and girlfriends, never with great success. Some jokes you had to grow up with. Anytime an old acquaintance came up in conversation, someone who'd followed a bad path and dropped off the map, one of them would inevitably conclude, "I don't know, man. I guess he went to Nebraska."

Even halfway across the state, JT still hadn't trusted his eyes. Though Omaha had resembled a real city after the dull plains of Iowa, I-80 funneled them into a wasteland. Mammoth skeletons of farm machinery loomed over acre after dry acre.

He knew the state could not all be one big parched cornfield. Nebraska was prime beef country, no less than Iowa. The interstate stood on a crucial stretch of the old Union Pacific Line and the Oregon Trail before that, but staring out into the void, JT marveled that any prospector or pioneer who'd reached this point could bear to go on. He would have gone cannibal long before Donner Pass.

Now, in revenge for his contempt, Nebraska was asserting its existence all over them.

"Look," Bobby said to the shop owner. "We came in and had some ice cream. Now we've got to go."

JT pulled the man aside. "What the hell is going on?" he asked.

The look the man gave him showed embarrassment, almost physical pain. He lifted his hand as Bobby, Lisa, and Katy hurried outside, hoping to stop them. They darted for shelter inside the camper.

"JT?" called Bobby.

JT sneered at the old man and called back, "I'll be right there." He waited for a silent moment.

The old man scratched the back of his withered-apple skull. "I just… You folks were so friendly to stop. I hate asking."

JT threw his hands up. "Oh, for…what? You want some of our beer? We don't have any weed. Or do you just want a lift out of Hell, Nebraska?"

The old man was close to tears. He blubbered something too quiet to hear.

"What is it?" asked JT.

"My dog."

JT was glad the others had gone ahead. The mention of animals in need was a sure trigger for Katy to lose it. Even JT could not repel a pang of dread. The old man composed himself with a long sigh.

"Your dog?" said JT. "Your dog wants a ride out of here?"

"My dog's poorly. He got hurt real bad. I need somebody to put him down. It's a sin watching him suffer, but I've had him so long I can't stand to, myself."

JT studied the man, looking for signs of some joke. The man's face was steady, but his eyes went to the dirt. Irritation dropped JT's voice into a snarl. "So, you invited us into this busted-ass sideshow for a sick dog?"

"He ain't… He's hurt something awful."

"Whatever!" JT said. "If he's hurt, if he's sick, do him a favor and just put him down. What kind of thing is that to ask a stranger?"

"I wouldn't never ask, but…"

"Look, obviously things aren't going great for you, but I never heard anything like this. Kill your own damn dog. Or if you really can't stand it, I'm sure that ugly character over there would be happy to oblige!"

He pointed across the road, but the smiling drunk had vanished. The old man stared at the blank space with bovine eyes. He mouthed a silent syllable.

"Please."

Fed up with arguing, and possibly drawn by macabre curiosity, JT allowed the man to lead him around the back of the store. Dense unmown patches of weeds hid from the sun there, in the shade of a derelict fuel tank on high rusty legs. JT saw six or seven dark shapes from a good distance away. They were crows, matted and gristly beyond easy recognition but crows all the same. They hopped and flapped their black wings, muttering in a soft argument as they took turns picking at something in the grass.

JT gave the old man a look of curious disgust and got a shamefaced nod in reply. They moved closer.

The dog was a mongrel, on the large side but with a good mix of terrier, so that even in the bloom of health its proportions would have been somewhat odd. It lay prone in the grass, so JT saw its rear legs and tail twitch in feeble agony. He also saw the wounds down its back and flanks, where sharp beaks and talons had torn away flesh. The dog put up a faint whine, lifting its head toward its master.

Nausea rose in JT's throat when he saw the ragged crater the birds had made of its right eye socket. The crows carried on bickering, unmindful of its pain.

"For the love of God," JT moaned.

"Just come out of the sky and took after him," the old man said, scratching harder at his bandage. "Never saw anything like it before, but ol' Tompall's been slowing up a lot. I tried to scare 'em off him but they got nothing else to eat in this drought. No corn growing."

"So kill the crows. Don't let them do...that to your dog." JT could barely look.

The old man shook his head. He could not look at all. "I kilt one with a shovel, broke the wing on another, but they come after me too." He quit scratching the wound on his arm and clutched it hard, squeezing until the pain showed on his face.

"I took one or two out and three new ones showed up that same day. They always been devil birds. Now something mean's took ahold of 'em."

"What in the almighty hell are you trying to say?" JT asked him.

"Deadly times. The good in things is all dried up. We never did have a year like this."

Unable to summon a reply, JT stalked back to the camper. Throwing the door open, he found Bobby handing out beers.

Lisa cracked hers and downed it with vigor. Katy held a cold unopened can against the back of her neck.

The bang of the door made Bobby jump and slop a billow of foam down his front. JT climbed inside and made straight for the built-in footlocker at the end of his bunk.

"Hey there," Bobby called. They were laughing off their weird encounter. "Beer for the driver? On the house, but you gotta tip me."

JT said nothing as he tossed aside a stack of towels and pulled a shotgun from the bottom of the well. His father's Browning pump-action 20-gauge was the only heirloom he had kept. He had learned to shoot with that gun, and it had done fine for the limited shooting his life required him to do.

"JT?" Katy whispered, leaning in his direction. "What's wrong?"

"It's fine," JT said quietly. "I'm coming right back."

"Aren't we going?" Lisa asked, glancing at Bobby.

"Sure we are," Bobby said with careful slowness. "Right, JT?"

"Everybody stay put for five minutes," JT said with no air left in his lungs. He fished out a loose shell and slipped it into his pocket. He knew better than to load the chamber. The sound of a pump action had the universal effect of spooking bystanders.

"Where are you going with that?" Katy pressed with unusual sharpness.

Bobby had a hand out.

JT ignored it. He looked his brother hard in the eye. "It's okay," he said. "I promise. Don't let them come outside."

The old man stood groaning where JT had left him, holding his head like a wounded simpleton.

"Here," said JT, offering the gun. "Loaded and ready. Make it a head shot."

The man did not move his arms to take the weapon. His

eyes were wide with impotent grief. JT did his best to be gentle. "It ain't my dog, mister. It's yours."

The old man shook his head, uncannily like a child.

"I couldn't. I'd miss. I wouldn't want to, but I'd make myself."

JT made a disdainful sound, pushed the man aside, and moved a step forward. The motion of shouldering the gun, practiced but long neglected, brought up memories JT would sooner not have tied to this day. His heart pulsed in the grip of an angry fist.

He was already squeezing the trigger when Bobby strode around the corner of the building, baseball bat in hand, braced for action. JT had no time to explain the situation or stop the movement of his finger. The blast of the shotgun, and what it did to the dog, said all there was to say.

CHAPTER THREE

Commotion

JT had his beer. He was not in the habit of drinking behind the wheel, but he granted himself a special dispensation, and none of his passengers objected. Over the next few miles, which seemed to last for days, drinking was the logical pastime. Conversation in the camper had ceased by unspoken agreement.

JT could feel the eyes on his back. Bobby would be staring in bemusement, coming off the shock of seeing his brother blow a hole in living matter for the first time in two decades. Lisa was less of a known quantity. He liked her fine and she seemed like a sport, but she was new to the family battlefield. Katy was the only one giving off hot rays of reproach. Her self-mastery would break before long, he reckoned over another sip from the can already warm in his grip.

JT and Katy had been married for three years, and as good as married a while longer. They had met through mutual friends in Shreveport, where Katy majored in sociology at Centenary with a religion minor. JT managed a busy landscaping crew, grabbing the units for a business certification at the local Remington campus whenever he could afford it. It turned out they had grown up less than fifty miles from each other in Texas.

Katy had chosen her school partly to maintain ties to her people in Nacogdoches, while JT had deliberately ventured beyond his family's reach. He had left home, a no-future town called Thaxtrom, shortly after his seventeenth birthday, still writing to his mother but more or less keeping radio silence where his father and brother were concerned. He and Katy understood and challenged each other, compensating for each other's shortcomings.

Katy had grown up kind, compassionate, and honest. She

shrank from undue self-assertion or confrontation. Her dream had been veterinary medicine, and she spent the summer before her junior year of high school as an animal clinic volunteer. Checking up on well animals suited her fine, but tending to ill or suffering ones proved too much for her tender heart to bear. This embarrassing letdown she shared only with JT.

Once, when they were both drunk on tequila following a Galveston beach concert, Katy had given him more of the story. The doctor in charge of her clinic, Talbot or Tobin or something, had been a cold customer with a hard-on for hectoring his assistants, especially the women. JT knew that medicine, like law enforcement, attracted the power-hungry, and this veterinarian had sounded to him like a classic workplace bully with a side order of intellectual vanity.

As soon as he clocked Katy's special sensitivity to animal suffering, the doctor had enlisted her to help with every euthanasia case that came into the clinic. Katy had tried thickening her skin, understanding that death would be a regular part of caregiving, but the doctor had made every possible effort to keep her away from the more gratifying, life-affirming parts of the job. She'd spent most of two months holding sick animals as they died, while the doctor spent more time studying her reactions than he did ensuring the quickest, most humane procedures possible for his little patients.

The rest of the story, hiding in plain sight, was that the doctor had picked on Katy especially. Perhaps he had groped or propositioned her outright, and his campaign to spoil any joy she took in the job had been revenge for her turning him down. If not, then daily abuse of authority had been enough to service his needs. Either way, he'd vampired every drop of her enthusiasm for animal care as a profession.

Since meeting JT, she'd taken in a number of stray pets, with the understanding that JT would deal with serious injury or sickness, letting her know as few details as possible.

JT was capable of great gentleness with animals, while his upbringing had left him guarded and prickly when it came to human beings. He hadn't whipped many asses in his life, but when he had to, he made an ass-whipping count. Once, it had nearly made a murderer of him. As a high school junior he'd beaten the piss out of a neighbor boy named Kenny Chase, with good reason but without any mitigating sense of control.

Kenny had been the kid brother of Marla Chase, a sophomore blessed with precocious curves and a pleasingly coarse mind. While not JT's first love, she'd been his first lover, and the mutual disapproval of their families only made the passion hotter while it lasted.

The Chase family had lived on a swath of county land unfit for most uses, downwind from a paper mill and adjacent to a water treatment plant. Most households on that side of town, including JT's family, had been poor, but the Chases were the neighborhood's designated trash. Their father, not an employee of either establishment befouling the local air, was home on some oilfield disability pension and dedicated all his free time to being a mean, shitty drunk. JT had borne no such prejudice against Marla, who shared his interest in Marlboros, music and clandestine sex.

A key impediment to their private happiness had been Kenny, the model of semi-rural adolescent mediocrity. A nose-picking loner who compulsively sketched violent pornography in the margins of school notebooks, Kenny tagged along anytime he spied JT and Marla together. Marla dismissed it as typical sibling behavior, but JT intuited what the boy was desperate to witness. It was not much of a secret how the couple spent their time, and JT suspected Kenny of attempting to graduate from peeping on his sister in the bathroom to watching her in a full-fledged bone session with an upperclassman.

Kenny's lurking presence and creepy habits hadn't been

enough to turn JT against him, until he discovered their true depth. One afternoon JT had recognized the kid's bike lying by the roadside at the edge of the pine woods. He'd only meant to check on Kenny as a favor to Marla, and would offer help or a ride if the little dickhead needed it. A short distance into the trees, he'd found Kenny hiding in an abandoned deer blind, performing amateur vivisection on a small spaniel he'd caught. A shallow pit, hastily dug and covered with wire mesh, held two half-flayed squirrels and a starved-looking kitten which the boy had evidently meant to torture next.

That moment of discovery was JT's first recollection of the sickness he felt watching a creature suffer needless cruelty. He had not bothered asking questions before he pulled Kenny to his feet by the neck of his t-shirt. He'd started hitting, and hadn't stopped for a long time.

He might have been able to justify the assault, except for the coup de grace which he regretted immediately and every day after. As Kenny dry-heaved and cried on the ground, JT had grabbed a can of lighter fluid from his glove compartment, drizzled it generously over the boy's head, and threatened to set him ablaze with a drugstore Bic. In the moment, JT had seen it as an apt lesson in how not to treat one's fellow creatures. In retrospect, he could scarcely believe how bugass crazy he'd gone.

With age came the realization of how many strings JT's parents must have pulled to keep him out of prison, and the incident had done nothing to foster warm feelings between him and his father. Luckily JT had been itching to leave home on account of unrelated domestic tensions. Once Marla told him to fuck off – there was no guessing what Kenny had told her when he arrived home, bloody and stinking of butane – JT had reckoned that ties with home were fully cut and he could begin the process of finding a better life elsewhere. Only later would he realize what a disservice that attitude had been to poor, confused brother Bobby.

The roadside merchant with the dead dog could not have known any of this, and even Katy knew only JT's carefully self-edited version of the story. His life had made a rapid change for the better when he met her. Their mutual softening and toughening, coupled with a shared fanaticism for live music, good whiskey, and home cooking had forged a union transcending their obvious divergences in personality. Despite her reluctance to confront painful truths, she was perceptive to an alarming degree. She read JT's expressions and gestures like newsprint on his forehead. That she knew him so well drove him crazy with love, but also with private exasperation. Their natural intimacy came with near-constant friction, typically manifesting as a low-key battle of wills. A fight with raised voices or long silences was a rare and serious occasion for them. JT worried that the day still had room for both extremes.

He concentrated on the taste of stale hops, and when the beer was done, he played a little one-man game called "count the cost." He used the speedometer and the time between telephone poles to calculate the acreage of every cornfield they passed, then estimated the yearly losses of each landowner by the volume and density of dead, looming crops. Here and there stood empty posts, probably where scarecrows had hung until they rotted away or defeated landowners took them down. Those counted for bonus points. If JT were on the road with different friends, maybe just with Bobby, the grim humor of the game might have thawed the atmosphere. He decided against sharing his fun because Katy, for one reason or another, would refuse to find it funny.

As if reading his thought, she lifted the speech ban. "You could have offered to take the dog to a vet."

JT slammed his empty can into the holder hard enough to buckle it. "A vet?"

"Like a farm vet, even. There has to be one somewhere near here."

JT's grip made the vinyl squeak on the steering wheel. "As if that has anything remotely to do with the point! Can we just leave it all here with the rest of this godforsaken state?"

"I don't think you had any right."

"Right? Forget right, somebody had a responsibility."

Katy sniffed. "You?"

"Not just me, Your Honor! Anybody!" said JT. "I told the guy a dozen times I had no right, and he had no right asking. Right and wrong was over and done with!"

Katy shifted in her seat. "So you shot the dog anyway, got back on the road? It didn't seem like a tough call for you."

"Oh, you don't think so? Tell you what, let me know when it starts getting through to you that the only harder thing for me than pulling that trigger was standing by and listening to a hurt dog moan?"

Katy had no reply for that, but she gave no gesture of concession. Her scowl deepened from anger to sorrow.

"You're sure it was suffering, though?" Bobby asked quietly. "Like, really done for?"

JT almost ignored him, but then didn't. "Hell, Bobby. I guess it's not for me to say. Seeing as I've done and said every wrong thing since I woke up today, I'm probably looking at this all wrong too. But if you ever see me slashed open with rabid hogs fighting over gobbets of me, I hope you'll have the sack to finish me off before they do."

"You never said about there being hogs," Lisa said, sounding sincerely confused.

"He's being gross," Katy huffed. "It was a bunch of stupid birds."

Lisa shook her head and scooted away toward her bunk.

"Katy," JT shot back with a twinkle of sardonic glee, "that dog didn't think they were so stupid. That old man didn't think they were stupid. Those birds were in charge of the situation!"

"Until you arrived. Our hero. Everybody's hero!"

"I'll take that, thank you very much."

"Fine! Hang it on your stupid-ass wall!" Katy seldom lost her temper, and saved even mild swearing for special occasions.

"Look…lady," said JT, suppressing a laugh, "you're the one who begged me to stop in the first place. You got out of the camper. All of you did! At least Bobby bought some ice cream off him. But I'm the one he asked for help. Not you. You asked me to help him, and then he asked me to help him, and help he got."

Hardheaded people have a special talent for making things worse in a stalemate. Their standard behavior when cornered is to martyr themselves lavishly, ensuring general as well as personal misery. In the heat of resentment, JT was surprised by a hand-painted sign he had not expected to see. He made a decision.

"Fine, if I'm such a drag on everyone's good vibrations, how about we stop and shop for some firecrackers?"

"Huh?" said Bobby. He'd been bugging JT about this for days, but the corn museum had dislodged it from his mind.

FIREWORKS AHEAD, the sign declared. Below the words, a crooked stick-figure rodeo clown rode a giant bottle rocket bronco-style.

Katy snorted. "Now you want to relax and have fun?"

He ignored her.

Bobby pointed at the sign. "I'll be damned. I knew it, a sign from God."

"A sign from the arts and crafts room at the state hospital," JT countered.

"Lisa, put your shoes back on!" Bobby called.

"What the hell for?"

When Bobby told her, she blew a dismissive raspberry.

"Are fireworks even legal in Nebraska?" Katy asked.

Bobby shrugged. "You think the highway patrol set up a sting?"

JT savored the silence when Katy didn't answer. She could only summon mild irritation at Bobby. He'd become like the kid brother she never had. Privately, JT figured that the stop would be a bust which nobody could hold against him. Judging from the condition of the sign, if anyone had sold fireworks on that road in the last fifty years, they'd probably been dead for ten.

"I bet we can clean them out for a song," Bobby said. He considered himself a top-notch negotiator in the fireworks market, ever since he was twelve. JT had never had the heart to explain that having a keen eye for cheap-ass products was not the same thing. But rich or poor, the brothers had always gathered fireworks when they could, for any special occasion.

Bobby hooted, pointing, as a pair of dull structures appeared on the roadside up ahead, with scant but unmistakable signs of human occupation. JT no longer felt smug. Tradition came around to bite them in the ass once more, and this time he had himself to thank.

The words DEE-LUXE FIREWORKS were stenciled above the window in blistered purple house paint. The stand had one adjacent structure, a dented Airstream serving as the proprietor's residence. An immense oldish woman wearing a green visor and huge boxy sunglasses sat outside the trailer on a precarious folding chair, chain-smoking. Colorful tattoos on her shoulders and bosom sagged out of all recognizable form. Her husband, or maybe brother, a shirtless barefoot sasquatch type about her equal in rough road miles, tended a tottering charcoal grill. The man glanced reluctantly at Bobby sidling up to the window, his hand raised in folksy greeting.

The woman stared at the road, paying them no mind until her dog, a geriatric beagle gone morbidly fat, wriggled from the shade under the Airstream and galloped toward them, wheezing in fury.

"Lightnin'!" called the woman. "Be quiet, Lightnin'!"

The dog shut up but waddled in circles around the interlopers. His growls were feeble hisses.

The man took his time wiping his hands on his short pants while he trudged up the ramp into the side entrance of the firecracker shed. The assortment of goods looked like the basic bait-shop inventory. Bobby made a big show of checking things over. Katy had stayed in the camper to enjoy some quiet time. Lisa hung back near the shoulder of the road. JT stood with her, arms folded, watching Bobby like a bored zoo patron.

"Look at him," said Lisa. "He's bouncing like a kid."

"Way to choose a man, Lisa," said JT, but with a grin.

"You think that lady's blind?"

"If she is," JT said, "I'm sure she can still hear you."

Lisa blushed, but the woman gave no sign of seeing or hearing them.

"Maybe the dog sees for her, like a witch's cat," JT said.

"You think the dog can see?" Lisa said, giving herself a fresh case of the giggles.

The old hound took offense, warbling out its feeble spite.

"Lightnin', hush!" said the woman, not breaking her oracle's pose.

A door opened on the side of the Airstream and a beefy kid emerged with a squat metal tank under his arm. He wore a stained coverall but was a decent copy of the shirtless fireworks man, add one generation of diluted chromosomes. His brow jutted an inch farther out, giving him a permanent surly face. He knelt beside the trailer, fumbling with some sort of propane valve, making a lot of rattle and fuss over swapping the tanks. JT did not realize he was staring until the kid turned and caught him.

They exchanged a long, unloving look, then JT offered a faint smile. "Never could work those damn fittings myself. Gonna have some cold nights in the mountains."

The boy considered this, then spouted a long stream of tobacco sludge. He stood and shuffled a few steps toward them. JT noticed the heavy adjustable wrench in his hand. Appraising the big city folks' camper, the young man gave a look that said JT was full of it, the thing probably ran on sunshine and spider webs.

Instead, the boy asked, "Wherzzat yer headed to?"

"Colorado," JT said. He regretted having started the conversation but reached for friendly common ground. "Do some fishing with my brother here."

The kid scrunched his face. Did they have water in Nebraska? "What's wrong with the fishin' where y'come from?"

Lightnin' punctuated the question with a snarl full of phlegm.

"Lightnin'!" Big Momma hollered.

JT was not sure how to answer the kid. "Not as hungry," he ventured.

"Hey, speaking of hungry," Lisa blurted, "you sure have some badass big crows around here. Do you have any problems with them being pests?"

JT gave her a dirty look.

She shrugged at him. Conversation under stress was not one of her strengths.

The kid studied them for half a minute, glanced at Bobby and Poppa No-Shirt. JT's attention settled on the Airstream, which had rusty-looking junk and garbage piled on its roof.

The kid turned his back and shambled away, sparing them further conversation. JT looked at Bobby, who was engaged in an animated chat with his host. The firecracker man was barely tolerating it.

"Got a case of these same pop rockets one time in Onalaska, Texas. Only sixty bucks down there."

"That so," said the man. "Alaska, huh." He spoke his questions without question marks.

"No, see, it was in Texas, but the town's called… Anyway, better get some Roman candles too."

A pack of brightly colored wands dropped on the counter. "Any M-80s?"

"Just what you see, son."

JT was about to intervene when Katy shrieked inside the camper. JT and Lisa traded a look, then JT reached for the door. He barely had it open when Katy bowled him over. She was still getting her arms into a t-shirt.

"JT, somebody was looking in at me!"

JT blinked, bewildered. "What are you talking about?"

"I was changing my shirt! I sweated through the other one. I pulled this one over my head and there's some weirdo standing at the window on the far side, gawking. What are you guys all doing out here anyway, having lunch or—?"

They jumped as a shower of small explosions burst the air around them. Bobby had thrown a potent string of crackers at their feet. He was doubled over with the cackles. The vendor stood watching, hold the amusement. Lightnin' trembled in the grass, pissing down his fleshy leg.

"Free sample," said Bobby. "I'll be sure and get some more of these!"

"Damn you, Bobby!" JT growled. "Get your shit and load up now."

"Aw, come on," said Bobby, missing the point. "I was only messing around."

The kid in the coverall came clomping around the back of the camper. He headed for the Airstream, where JT had thought he already was, without paying the slightest attention to the others. He exchanged a momentary look with his father, then spat again. The ugly brown stream just missed the toe of his work boot.

"Hey!" JT yelled. "Hey, what's your problem, Deliverance?"

JT went for the kid, heedless of the big wrench he still swung in one hand. Lisa yanked him back with surprising reflexes and strength. Bobby jogged over to help her. The kid bounded up the steps of the Airstream and disappeared inside.

The shirtless man looked at Bobby, unimpressed with the chaos. "How 'bout you take what you bought and keep moving." Again, not a question.

A poultry truck, stacked with cages of squabbling hens, blew past on the highway. The foul stench wafting behind it seemed a final sign that it was time to go. JT weighed his anger against attacking a family of early hominids on their home turf, threw up his hands, and herded the women into the camper.

"Bobby," he said, not turning around.

Bobby left some cash without waiting for change and scooped up his armful of purchases. Nobody mentioned the incident as they put the next ten miles behind them.

Bobby admired his haul. "If the fish don't bite," he said, to break the awkward hush, "we'll blow 'em out of the water."

Nobody answered him. Katy smoldered in her seat, and Lisa was busy attacking some crackers and pepperoni. JT itched with the anticipation of an old argument ready to blaze up again. In his eagerness to pre-empt the talk, he chose his words without much thought.

"I'm sorry about all that, hon. That kid grew up east of jackshit, got a few short wires to boot. He's probably never seen a real live woman before."

She sniffed. "Now you're blaming me for—"

"I'm not blaming you for anything, Katy! What are you blaming me for?"

"JT, nobody blames you," Lisa snapped. Her cheerful patience was cracking. Katy echoed her more faintly. Her eyes said, "You know why," but her mouth said "I'm not…"

"Look, you can rag me for being a tight-ass or a stick in the mud, because damn it…I'm road weary like all of us. Or you can be on my case for trying to make my little brother happy. Just make up your mind what you're mad about."

"How about for this whole detour through the buttcrack of nowhere?" Katy said quietly. "Maybe next time we can vote on things like abandoning the highway?"

"How about dead and suffering dogs?" JT said it without thinking. "Can we abandon them, at least?"

"Hey," Bobby said, "not cool."

Katy shook her head. "That's not fair."

JT bit back another tirade. "Fine, but if we're being fair, that's the one thing I won't have anyone blaming me for. That's all. If you think I did the wrong thing, put in an extra prayer for me tonight."

"Like that would help."

Katy stared out the passenger window, her arms folded so tightly that her shoulders hunched. JT did not look at her, so he could not tell whether it was a stubborn jab intended to further ice him out or the kind of crack that would force them both to smile and start the reconciliation. Katy was a soft touch in many respects, but she stashed resilient jabs for when JT's guard was down.

JT decided to resist, in case he was wrong. "I'm done. No longer interested. Anybody else wants to discuss it, pass notes."

Katy got out of her seat and headed for the rear cabin. JT could barely hear her but thought she said, "I'm going to lie down." JT gave a curt nod that could mean anything but was calculated to mean nothing.

When he turned in his seat a few minutes later to check the rear cabin, he saw her pale blue sock feet protruding from the end of the bunk. She was tall, but had never learned to tower over people in an advantageous way.

Lisa and Bobby had been whispering, a conversation that ended with Lisa giving an unconcerned shrug. Bobby got up to make his way to the passenger seat as she slipped on her headphones. JT could hear a tiny buzzing rendition of something broad and twangy with lots of guitars. Brooks & Dunn probably. Maybe George Strait, if her taste ran slightly older. Only in the last while had JT begun to suspect Lisa showed a mere fraction of what went on in her head. If she turned out to have Crystal Gayle or Sir Douglas in her stack of music, he might regret never having asked her out.

"Don't worry about it," Bobby murmured, sliding into the seat.

"Don't plan to," JT said. They had a motto in their family: Have a beer and forget about it. For the many ways it had shaped their lives, both wonderful and disastrous, JT could picture it printed on their family crest.

"Take it easy on her. She'll get over it," Bobby said.

"Possibly. Anyhow, she'll stow it somewhere when she wakes up. Ain't matrimony grand?"

"Couldn't say, but it looks like a riot," said Bobby with a faint smile. He paused, waiting to see if JT would needle him about getting married, but that was not where the topic turned. One side of Bobby's grin drew down.

"You okay, bro?"

"What kind of man," JT demanded as though Bobby had not been speaking, "asks another man to kill his dog? We should have kept driving, just get where we're going."

"Look," Bobby said, popping another beer for himself, "that whole scene back there was no bueno. All right? Bad call by the group. But if we're not gonna stop except for gas and eats, why didn't we just fly to Colorado?"

"What, live out of our carry-on bags and shave kits?"

"Hell, for the money we're spending on gas for this monster, we could buy some cheap tents and a camp stove, and pocketknives and some new trout poles. Besides the bunks and the locking doors, which I admit are very nice, what could we not have taken along that we'd really want?"

JT thought immediately of the shotgun, and the baseball bat.

"It wouldn't have been right," was the only answer he could find. "Flying into Denver and renting a van, that's tourism. To hell with that. It's not the trip we planned."

"For what it's worth, I agree. And sure, this part of the country turned out to be kind of a bummer, but that's the experience. I mean hell, we're still seeing it, aren't we? Places none of us have been."

"We should have come sooner, then. Before the heartland had a coronary."

Bobby laughed, but he shook his head. "What did you expect it to be like? Stagecoaches and whiskey boats?"

"Shit, Bobby, I don't know. Folks getting by with more dignity than this. How about a little bit of frontier resourcefulness?"

"I maybe wouldn't judge the whole territory on a few sun-crazy yokels."

They whizzed past a few telephone poles. JT had lost his pleasure in reckoning how dead the corn belt was. Both women were in their bunks. They did not snore with the ferocious energy of the men, but neither was as ladylike in sleep as she might have wished.

Bobby wrestled with some thought.

"What?" JT asked.

"Nothing, just…" He peeked over his shoulder. "Lisa's kinda up and down. Hope she's not coming down with something."

JT thought that would be the end of the talk for a while, but Bobby went on.

"So, that dog, what do you think? Did a car hit it or what?"

"Hell if I know. Old fool probably ran his mower over it. Or a couple coyotes ganged up on it last night. It was all beat to hell somehow and couldn't do nothing but lie there and cry. Made me want to puke."

"He didn't say how the dog got hurt? The old guy?"

"He's a loon, Bobby. Doesn't know the sky from his asshole. He tried to sell me this line about these birds gone, like, psycho carnivore."

"Birds? What do you mean?"

"I mean some crows were pecking on the dog while it died, and he's convinced they're to blame."

"They were trying to eat it alive?"

"Well, barely alive, but yes, I guess so. Of course they're going to eat once the meat stops moving. They're not pack hunters."

Bobby thought about this, and JT enjoyed the brief silence. Both were surprised when Lisa piped up, still reclining and muffled.

"Those other folks back there sure didn't want to talk about crows."

"I thought you were asleep," Bobby said.

"Nope. Thinking."

"The way they'd rigged up the trailer…" JT said. "You saw

that too?"

Lisa looked blank. "Nope, just the way that father and son looked at each other when I mentioned it. Like we were suddenly a bad scab that needed picking off."

"Yuck," said Bobby. "What was up with their trailer? You mean all that gnarly Road Warrior business on top?"

JT nodded.

He had at first dismissed it as a primitive artistic expression. At second glance, it was an ordered array of razor wire, jagged sheet metal, and smaller debris like bent silverware and tin can lids. He had seen the same thing at bus stops in Houston and once on the train in Chicago. Cities put spikes on eaves and ledges to keep pigeons from roosting and crapping everywhere. Those people had fixed their home to keep winged visitors from landing, and with truly nasty conviction. Just looking at it had made JT think about a bad case of blood poisoning. He was on the verge of testing his home defense theory with the others when Lisa steered the conversation aside.

"How come there weren't any bigger birds?" Lisa was into bird watching, wildlife hikes, all that business, and it had rubbed off on Bobby. His photo hobby matched up with her tattered field guides and bird journals. This had been a selling point for the Colorado trip. It also meant one of them was always ready to add some weird nature factoid to a conversation, whether or not it fit the occasion.

The angry blare of a horn brought JT's attention back to the road. Before his mind could make sense of what he saw, he brought the wheel right as quickly as he could without losing control. The honker was a red sedan in the oncoming lane, swerving nearly off its own side of the road as it howled past. At first, JT thought he was drifting, but the car had been honking at a mud-caked pickup that roared up abreast the camper to pass. It could have been a grisly three-car smash had the smallest of the three not vacated the road.

"Son of a bitch," JT said almost under his breath.

"Everyone around here's a maniac," said Bobby.

JT was inclined to agree. He checked his side mirror carefully before settling fully back into his lane.

Bobby blinked. "What were we talking about?"

"Birds," Lisa said. "Other birds besides crows. A dead dog—or a dying one, anyway—would draw vultures for miles."

JT nearly snapped back that there had been vultures. There had, but not near the fuel tank or the dog. They had been across the road, waiting on something else out in a field to die. Or else waiting their turn on the dog.

"So what," JT asked instead, "you think the crows put the whammy on all the other scavengers? Made them scared to come up on a kill?"

Lisa sat up and shrugged. "Crows and ravens are about as smart as birds get. In a starvation crisis, I don't see why they couldn't mount some kind of organized aggression."

"You mean like a beehive, or like the Third Reich?" JT did not bother hiding the roll of his eyes.

"Seriously," said Bobby, excited, "when there's not enough food, things change. Animals adapt, especially the sharp ones like crows. Yeah, crows! Sure, they use tools and everything."

"These were the regular kind," said JT. "No knives and forks. I also thought we agreed to drop this conversation."

"You'd be surprised," Bobby said. "Lisa, what was that show we saw? They had these crows in a lab, making tools out of sticks and paper clips to get at food."

"I wish you could hear yourselves," JT said with sudden heat. "You're a couple of nutcases, and I'd sincerely rather drive the camper into a tree than talk about this anymore today!"

"JT, stop yelling at everyone!" Katy called from the back of the van.

"I am not yelling!" he roared.

"Well, you woke me up!"

"Maybe you nagged yourself awake."

"All righty," Bobby said, rousted out of his good humor. "Everyone chill your asses out. JT, it's time for me to drive for a while."

"Great," JT said through his teeth, braking hard. "You just enjoy it. Only, make sure if you see a piece of roadkill, let Katy out to nurse it better."

"No thanks," Katy said, "I wouldn't want to get shot!"

JT was gathering himself to unleash hell for the fifth or sixth time that day when he caught a moving object in the side mirror. He was braced for another white-knuckle overtake, but the battered black pursuer vehicle settled behind him, keeping pace.

"No," JT said, forbidding the universe to taunt him further.

The party lights came on, blue and red.

JT would not have taken it for a police vehicle, but it made sense that the local state patrol would be outfitted with last decade's damaged equipment. He drifted the camper to the side of the road in a sort of trance. He had a vague awareness of Bobby and Lisa asking him questions, but his mind did not receive them. He heard the gratifying sounds of aluminum cans being scooped up and hastily hidden. He needed a little teamwork.

"Tell Katy," he said to nobody in particular, "if she wants to shoot me, now would be an okay time."

CHAPTER FOUR

You Ain't Going Nowhere

The trooper, badly shaven and a shade too bulky for his uniform, had the same ramshackle look as his car. His hat was the neatest thing about him.

"Have you done any drinking today?" he asked without much apparent interest in the answer.

"I had a beer with lunch."

"With lunch or for lunch, sir?"

JT sighed. "Two beers and a cheese sandwich for lunch."

The trooper arched his eyebrows.

"And some ice cream."

Lisa stifled a snicker, fortunately out of earshot. The trooper took a minute deciding whether JT was too much wiseass for his taste, but let it lie.

"The reason I stopped you," he said, "is on account of that broken taillight."

"The…what?" JT started to get up a little too quickly.

The officer assumed a warning stance.

JT threw his hands up and sat down again. "Sorry," he said. "Sorry. It's just, this is the first I've heard of a broken light."

"It's good and broken, all right. Smashed clean out. Were you in a collision today?"

"No, I'd definitely remember that."

"Didn't back up hard into any walls? When did you last inspect the vehicle for damage?"

"I don't…" JT stammered, because how the hell was he supposed to answer a question like that. "We gassed up and did the windows in…uh…"

"Kearney," Bobby offered.

"Kearney, yes, and everything was intact then."

"Have you stopped since then?" the cop asked.

"Yes, a couple of times… Just pee breaks and snacks."

The lawman, who presumably knew what lay between Kearney and their present location, looked skeptical.

"Is it okay if I get out and look?" JT asked.

"Who else is in the vehicle, sir?"

"My brother, his girlfriend, and my wife's laying down in the back. Do you want—"

"No, that's fine. You just have them stay put."

That made something in JT's guts tingle. He had never given much of a damn for cops in the first place, had never come out on the winning side of a traffic stop or fender bender, no matter how minor. He considered and discarded a couple of lighthearted comments, which might have eased his own mood but would not have warmed the atmosphere between them, as he exited the vehicle and followed the officer toward the back of the camper.

The damage was localized, ruling out JT's suspicion that he had scraped another vehicle without knowing it. The taillight was not cracked as he had pictured, but completely taken out as the trooper had said. The force of impact was sufficiently concentrated to smash the housing and the bulb as well.

The camper had picked up plenty of dust and road soot, but JT noticed another thing. The bumper on that side was flecked with brown, as if somebody had squeezed a cut finger over the chrome and let it dry in the sun. JT had seen stains like that a short time ago—not from blood but from low-grade chewing tobacco. He pictured the face of a troglodyte in coveralls waving a wrench, the dumb-looking creep who had scared Katy fooling around at the rear of the camper. His fists went a bloodless white.

"You don't recall anything that might have caused this?" the trooper asked.

JT weighed various explanations, but he could not articulate an account of the day's events that wouldn't sound crazy. He was certain the kid had put out his taillight in a chest-thumping display of meanness. But the part where he had peeked in on Katy was an embarrassment they would all sooner forget than dredge back up. Making the second stop had been JT's call, as if prior events had not been warning enough. For all he knew, the highway patrolman attended regular Sunday dinners with the Airstream clan. It would take so little for this day to complete its downward slide into every slasher movie JT had seen about cross-country travel. Why, he thought, did there have to be miles and miles of godless backcountry between any two desirable points on a map?

The trooper looked tired of jogging JT's memory. "You're gonna need that replaced immediately. Meantime, I reckon you better patch it with some reflective tape if you got it. Otherwise, get some. You follow me?"

JT nodded. He winced as the trooper scribbled a slip on his notepad, extended his hand in no hurry to take it. He blinked. "What is this?"

"This here is what we call a warning. If you get stopped again before you can fix the light, I can't say it'll help to flash this, but it can't hurt anything. So just fix it pronto, understand?"

"You're not gonna ticket me?"

"You done anything else I should know about?"

JT shook his head.

"Son, you seem like today's not been your best day, and I got a hunch you don't want to be driving this road any more than people like me want to see you here. Look after those folks of yours and drive careful."

JT fought the urge to throw his arms around the trooper and weep. That might have upset the tolerant goodwill between them. Somehow, he could not entirely believe that the cop, or that Nebraska, was letting him go. "I really appreciate that."

"I expect you do, and I'm gonna ask you one favor. If you

get to where you're going, either stay there or find some other way to come back. Your choice."

Though fairly certain he was not supposed to, JT put out his hand. "You won't see us again."

The officer considered the proffered hand, then shook it. "I guess that'll suit both of us fine."

JT savored his first break of the day, never mind the series of monumental missteps that had led him there. He could not even summon the anger from moments ago toward the boy who had vandalized the camper. Nebraska had chewed on them, but seemed more inclined to spit them out than swallow them. That was something at least, and he got to enjoy it for almost nine more miles.

The next man they saw in the middle of the road was dead, a slumped mass in jeans and a heavy work shirt. His haunches were high in the air, so his weight rested on his knees and forehead. He looked like he had died in a bizarre prayer to the oncoming traffic. A dark trail on the highway showed how he had flown clear of his pickup cab via the windshield and skidded where he landed, mostly on his face.

A hastily assembled road barrier blocked the camper from moving past. Just beyond, a pair of state cruisers sat with their doors agape and lights flashing. JT searched for the trooper he had just met, but the second-rate shave was not among the four faces present. Two stood over the body in the road, looking not too urgent about getting him some medical attention. There was clearly no point.

The poultry truck had turned over on its side. Its driver was not visible, but must have been somewhere under the half-crushed cab. More remarkable was the litter of overturned and split-open cages all across the highway and both shoulders. The snapped bars jutted like thorns from the wreckage. White feathers painted with blood and dust were everywhere, teased by breezes and floating to earth like snowflakes in hell.

"Highway's closed," was about the only information the sunburned lead cop would volunteer.

"Can't we get around?" said Lisa.

"Ma'am, highway's closed. We gotta clear this."

The road trippers had dismounted and gone to the edge of the barrier, compelled by the scene and the thought of how narrowly they had missed it. Katy had been forced to turn away when she saw a hen with broken wings try to squirm out of its open cage. Feeble peeps and clucks from dozens of injured fowl added to the queasy repugnance of the scene.

"Is someone gonna clear it?" Bobby asked, doubting the appropriate services existed in these parts.

"We got a call in," said the cop, who made a show of studying the sky as he spoke. "Gonna need all motorists to detour 'til the wreckers get in."

"And the medics!" Lisa added in her best helpful tone.

The cop did not bother responding. JT wondered what kind of expression hid behind the polarized shades. Katy, with one foot back inside the camper, said something under her breath. JT did not exactly hear it, but figured it must be, "How long will the wrecker take?"

"How soon do y'all usually clear a wreck like this?" JT asked.

The cop looked offended, as if JT meant to imply that deadly crashes were common on that straight stretch of minor highway. JT had meant to imply it.

"Mister, we got folks dead here and no way to move these vehicles at this time. I told you all motorists need to detour." He jerked his thumb at an orange sign with a big arrow pointing to the right, where a small farm road curved out of sight through a clump of cottonwood trees. The sign was rusty under the flaking paint and riddled with what looked like pistol holes. It had probably ridden around in a cop's trunk for fifteen years, rattling among other heavy-duty official junk waiting for days like this.

The other troopers were looking over now, their shared demeanor of boredom beginning to seem dangerous. JT's attention focused on three black birds that perched on the tipped-over truck. One put its beak between the bars of a cage, probing for the terrified flapping hen inside. Another made a sharp dive, intercepting an escaped pullet that tried to flee on one good leg. The third perched on the highest point of the flatbed, posted like a lookout. The crows were shaggy and unkempt enough to be buzzards, and almost big enough too, but they were not the meanest-looking specimens he had seen since breakfast.

The pickup's rear cab window was smashed. Bloody fangs of window glass winked from the frame. A fourth crow emerged from the jagged hole like a final clot coughed up by the dead truck. It swooped low over the road and perched on the dead driver's haunch, where it pecked indecently until the nearest of the cops removed his hat to swat the thing away. Lisa groaned in disgust as it circled upward and away over the roof of the camper.

The public relations cop had lost the last of his patience. "Sir," he said in an official tone, almost shouting, "I need you to move that vehicle out of here."

JT heard a soft retch behind him. Turning, he expected to see Katy taking a knee, bracing a hand against the camper. The atmosphere was on the verge of making him sick, so she was doubly pardoned. Instead, pink shoes revealed that Lisa was the one yacking in the weeds. That threw JT. Lisa had been prone to spells of listlessness and carsickness, but she had seemed better equipped than Katy to witness carnage and suffering.

"Hey, shithead!" the cop growled, moving a hand to his firearm. "You and your party board the vehicle and proceed on your way."

That got them moving.

Almost everything JT and company encountered that day had managed to enrage or upset him. But the wreck was the first thing to cross a line and spook him. He had lost too many friends to drunk drivers, icy roads, and the other dirty twists of fate dealt by the wondrous age of modern road travel. The aftermath of destruction would have stirred his heart in any case, but the calm of the scene before tow trucks and hearses and whatever else descended to sweep up the pieces, delayed by isolation and a general attitude of things getting done when they got done, had given him the stone-cold creeps.

He thought of the silent state troopers, how they could do nothing but poke and pick at the remains. Meanwhile, those morbid black birds made their own forensic studies with beating wings and hungry beaks as if they had some ownership over the catastrophe. The first comparison to cross his mind was nuclear testing. He knew next to zero about radioactive fallout, but he had read stories about roving packs of mad dogs in the Chernobyl ruins that somehow bred and marauded the area for generations.

Or had that been in a crummy midnight movie? It seemed a stretch for a toxic environment to turn one species monstrous while the rest of the ecosystem seemed normal. Drought-ridden and suicidally bleak, yes, but more or less normal.

Maybe some disease had affected them, some kind of avian hydrophobia that got into the water or the corn or who the hell knew what. He reflected on Lisa's lecture about crows and their smarts. If animal populations evolved, maybe a brainy bunch of crows in a compromised environment could adapt to climb a rung on the food chain. That was a scientific theory he decided to keep to himself. JT had what Taffy Whatsername in the Hitchcock movie never thought of: number-four birdshot, and a couple of slugs for good measure.

After so many detours and whiplash turns, JT doubted that the others would argue about making straight for the state line. They had three strikes with the local community. The inning was over. Nebraska had tried and rejected them, or vice versa. The brothers could return with clear consciences to thinking of the state as a dead hole in space, a drain for bad mojo.

He checked the fuel gauge and realized they would need to fill up promptly once they hit the state line. That was okay. Colorado would be a fresh page in the ledger. He vowed not to stop again for a hundred miles, believing he would get no argument from the others. They were all ragged and would sleep like the dead when the opportunity came. JT was eager to rest his own eyes, but would not surrender control of the wheel until the Nebraska misadventure was behind them for good.

The farm route took its sweet time finding a junction with another east-west road. JT was coming around to the idea that something meant to teach him a cosmic lesson in patience. He'd probably end up back at the interstate, a handful of miles from where they had left it hours ago, completing one jacked-up polygon of a wasted day. Then Katy had to pipe up and complete the thought for him, of course.

"I vote we stick to interstates from now on," she said. "Your shortcuts are for the birds."

It did not matter that she was right, or that she was trying to be funny, or that he was inclined to agree with her. It was like a psychic prank she played sometimes, and it drove him bonkers.

"I just knew we couldn't be done with this topic yet," JT said. "All I've heard today is how I need to loosen up and embrace the adventure. Well, as I recall, that's how today started—one little detour to get us on the right road."

"You know where the right road would have got us by now?" Katy snapped.

"Where?"

"Colorado!"

The perfect retort was cooking in JT's head when the camper began to shudder. Lisa and Bobby grabbed their bunks and each other to keep from falling. Bobby looked out the window frantically, as though he thought they might have hit the ocean somehow. JT clutched the wheel hard enough to crack the vinyl, let his foot off the gas, and held on as the vehicle's quaking peaked and faded.

Everyone noticed the distinctive slant of the floor. The right rear tire was out, and nobody dared say it out loud. JT considered laughing but could not bring his body to do it.

Cause of death was a no-brainer. JT and Bobby saw the galvanized head of a steel bolt, nearly an inch in diameter, poking from the tread. Where they had picked it up neither could say, but as Bobby worked it loose they discovered that it was close to seven inches long. Patching the tire was out of the question. The puncture was too wide for what they had on hand. It needed a full change.

Bobby whistled. "Some kinda day, huh, bro?"

A nasty heat glowed between JT's temples. He knew nothing about predestination or planetary alignments, but the day's misfortunes fed his conviction that some evil force in the universe had his number. He gave the tire a savage kick and stalked away toward a stand of trees.

"JT, what gives?" Bobby called. "Are we changing this thing or what?"

"Leave it! Just let me alone for a minute. I have to take a leak."

"Okay, you want me to get the jack out or—"

"Do what you want. Think for yourself!" JT bellowed. "I have to go over there and piss right fucking now!" He went, hurling more creative profanity into the sky.

Often in his life, usually following a colossal fight with his old man, JT believed with fervent hope that he had crashed to earth from some other planet. He knew better than to say this aloud. Even his mom and Katy—the two most compassionate women he had ever known—would tell him his hardheadedness proved beyond a doubt that he was his father's son.

As many miles as he put between east Texas and himself, as many troubled family links as he'd left there to rot, JT took pride in hailing from such dynamic roots in such a strange and distinctive place. A peculiar meeting of wildness and civilization lingered there, left over from the days of westward expansion, not just in the geography but in the attitudes of people who had shaped him. All his life he had lived among hunters, homesteaders, and self-sustaining pioneers. JT had added wanderer to that list, but he kept an essential connection to the rest of it. Even Dad, the contrary son of a bitch, had virtues he admired and hoped to inherit. The courage and good sense with which the old man tackled life's challenges had belied the narrow-minded coldness he reserved for interactions with his tribe.

An air force combat veteran and onetime pilot for the Strategic Air Command, JT and Bobby's father was a man of maddening utilitarianism. Having two sons grow up without a sense of constraint on their personal goals had been an anxious nightmare for him. Not that either of them had asked him for a dime since they were old enough to do a day's work. That was somehow not the point.

Mom said the bitterness between Dad and JT was really love so fierce it had swelled up and broken both their hearts. JT was far from certain about all that, but he would admit that he and his dad were at their most toxic when one was down and needed kind words, not kicks, from the other.

In the decade since he met Katy, JT had let some barriers down. He'd paid her the rare honor of bringing her to visit his extended family, and he'd made efforts beyond his own self-motivation to mend fences with Bobby. That had taken a while, since despite his natural good humor, Bobby clearly reckoned that he had been left to fend for himself in the chaotic household arena. Any resentment he'd nursed for his prodigal older brother – JT would damn well admit to being that – had dissolved under numerous drunk or half-drunk sentimental moments they'd shared.

Bobby had walked the line, kept his head down and his haircut clean for twenty-five years even though their dad's unforgiving scrutiny had driven both brothers equally crazy. JT was permanently temperamental and rough around the edges, resigned to being seen that way by others. Bobby kept his frustrations in a deep place under a calm business-casual demeanor. Though not fundamentally unhappy, he was desperate to please. He would always be known as the nicer brother and the life of the party, which truly he was, but in raucous moments of celebration JT could see strain in Bobby, a persistent anxiety of losing his cool over a tactless remark or a spilled beer, a critical loss by the home team. He was fearful of turning out too much like his father, and possibly his older brother.

He had never set out to find a calming feminine influence on his life, but he and Lisa had been going together longer than any previous relationship that JT knew about. Lisa had calibrated Bobby's oddball bachelor habits to a greater awareness of people around him. They had met at DePaul, where she was in a teaching program. Bobby's engineering firm had him on some job in Chicago for a few years, and on the side, he had taken some intro courses in photography. This awakened a latent passion that might one day threaten to overtake his sensible nine-to-five career.

The cross-country road trip had been a pet project of the two brothers for a long time, and finally the day had come to realize it. JT and Katy were settled in Virginia, working to save capital for a bed and breakfast they wanted to open on the coast. From boat repair and catering to pet grooming and hotel reception, they had tried nearly everything. JT was a worker bee, but never so much that he could not keep two or three bands going. He played keys and harmonica, two skills cultivated and calculated to make him attractive to almost any rock or blues group seeking part-time members. Long jams were his passion but so far not the source of any fortunes.

From his friend and current employer, the owner of a piano restoration and resale business, he had earned permission to borrow the camper and make the Colorado trek, stopping in Illinois for Bobby and Lisa. The destination was any friendly spot along the South Platte River, the ultimate aim a celebration of the wholesome industry, discipline, and self-sufficiency their father had taught them without the burden of his actual company over days and nights of travel. Like all good sons, they did their daily best, even as grown men, to strain out the bad advice, poisonous jealousy, and general peevishness that came pre-mixed with their father's work ethic and moral sense. This could be best achieved as many hundred miles away as possible from the old man himself.

JT knew, as Bobby must also have known, that despite these good days the two of them would have their share of cuss-fights yet. Not over anything important, because that was not how arguments worked. Their hereditary legacy of hot blood and stubbornness demanded it. Despite his satisfaction at putting their long-delayed adventure into action, JT had spent a thousand miles fighting a dull dread that they would soon reach the arena for that fight. That almost guaranteed Katy and Lisa's direct involvement, compounding the amount of shrapnel and the permanence of any wounds given. Things would be said that nobody could change or take back.

The lot where the camper sat did not belong to a farm. None of the brown overgrowth was corn or any recognizable crop. A large concrete foundation occupied the middle, torn away in chunks but intact enough to show the footprint of a large commercial building, from which not a scrap of wood or glass was left. It had probably been a feed store. A sapling tree had sprung up through one of the cracks. Looking closer, Bobby saw activity roiling on the slender trunk. A swarm of ants, their tiny bodies an angry red, surged up a thin channel cut in the bark.

At one fork a feeble branch had tried to grow. Nestled snugly in the fork were the wispy bones of a lizard, eaten away by the ravaging insects. It seemed to have been lifted from some death-metal album cover, good for a picture with the macro lens.

A few minutes later, Bobby found JT behind some high

weeds about a hundred and fifty yards from the road. With the trumpeting bull temporarily gone from the herd, the girls had decided to deal themselves a hand of poker in the shady, and more importantly quiet, refuge of the camper. Only Bobby had wanted fresh air.

"We could all use a break," Katy had said with an absent nod, though she must not have meant from the camper.

"Don't mind us, babe," Lisa had said. "Go get a nice relaxing heatstroke."

Now Bobby had a cool beer in his outstretched hand, the one commodity still in reasonable supply. The beer, not the ice, which meant it had to be cool instead of cold. JT took the can but let out a belch and stared at it without opening it.

"You all right?" Bobby asked, watching the horizon instead of his brother. It was their old way.

"Fine and dandy," JT said. "Alive and well in the Lord's country."

"Are we sure the Lord made this part?"

"I think there used to be the kind of person who could live in places like this and call it paradise."

"My goodness," Bobby said with a nervous chuckle, "don't tell me you're fixing to barf up thirty years of Dad talk now."

"He wasn't all wrong. Full of fertilizer, yes, but right about plenty of things too."

"Well, listen to you," Bobby almost whispered. Not sarcastic but surprised. Possibly impressed.

"You remember he always made us wring the neck of anything we wounded. Wouldn't lay a finger on anything we brought him unless it was dead."

In the same instant they both remembered squirrels, rabbits, and doves taken with pellet guns or the old single-shot .410 they had each used before graduating to heavier arms.

"Makes a boy careful about the shots he takes," Bobby said.

JT, he knew, had taken a different point from the lesson.

The brothers had argued about it before. Their father, JT would explain, had been a decent shot but no real marksman. Sure, if a wounded pig or a deer needed tracking, it was vital to bring it down as close and quickly as possible. As for smaller animals, their father had made no distinction between a bird brought down with two shots or with six, as long as it did not lie suffering for one second longer than necessary. Make a crack headshot and bully for you, but once you take the first shot nobody else in the world should have to finish the job.

Dad had not concerned himself with many of the basic sins advertised by the church. He drank and swore copiously, was quick to wrath, and held the music of Hank Locklin and Red Foley in nothing less than idolatry. The only sins he recognized were those of failed duty and neglected honor, always defined in his own terms. That narrow sense of principle gave him a violent aversion to any questioning of his orders. Bobby had observed some, but not all, of these traits in JT as the years wound on.

"It's about right and wrong," JT said. "But Katy's got this blind spot about helpless little things that—"

"Katy's got a big heart," Bobby said airily, bringing them back to the point. "Believe it or not, so do you. It just bleeds for different things. We're a long line of sentimental hard-asses."

JT smiled. "Bobby, I swear by holy smoke that all I want is to get this part of the trip over with. Once I'm stacking the brown trout, ankle deep in that frosty river, I promise I'll lighten up."

"Okay," said Bobby, pulling something from his pocket, "but nobody said you had to get us there all by yourself. The road is a big part of the road trip. The crappy days like this are gonna make good stories, even better than the good days maybe. Remember, we have to go back east at some point. There's no rule that says you can't have a laugh with the rest of us when things don't pan out like we wanted."

"Like Ogallala?" The interstate detour had nixed their plan to visit the town featured so heavily in Larry McMurtry's Lonesome Dove saga, which they'd worshiped (particularly the original novel) from boyhood.

"Exactly like Ogallala. Now, how about you listen to my plan."

JT folded his arms and gave Bobby his full attention.

"Today's a wash, no argument there. We've got plenty of snacks and beer to make a meal for the night. If we feel like working on the tire, we fix it. If not, we get a decent night's sleep, fix the son of a bitch at the crack of dawn, and get our buns to Colorado. We can all scratch an extra vacation day on the tail end. Any of us gets canned for that, we'll come back here and run the corn emporium."

JT snorted, then gave his brother's words a moment of serious reflection. "So tomorrow's a do-over. Hell with today."

"Now you've got it. Come on, spark one up and fucking forget about it."

JT arched his eyebrows, perhaps wondering whether Bobby had brought something along to smoke. Instead, Bobby held up a pair of bottle rockets he'd grabbed from the camper on the sly. It was an ancient pact sealer between them, one they had not used in a while. JT grabbed one and gave it a light. Bobby watched to see whether maturity had softened his brother, but JT held the wooden stem well past the danger point indicated on the label, until the primary fuse fizzed. When sparks charred his hand with soot, he tossed the rocket in the air and watched it spin in wild loops until it cracked open with a flash.

Bobby smiled. "Not bad. You could have gone longer."

"Yeah?" JT said. "Let's see that other one."

He snatched the rocket and lit it. This time he locked eyes

with Bobby, counting three seconds, four, and just when the warning fuse caught, he tossed it softly to about shoulder height between them.

Bobby half-dove, half skipped as the nose of the rocket glanced off his shoulder and zoomed past his ear. He heard JT hollering in a passable imitation of the old Airstream lady.

"Lightnin'! You, Lightnin', quit that barkin' and set your ass down!"

Bobby hit the deck. The rocket burst less than a foot above his head. "You dickhead," he mumbled into the ground without malice.

"Don't try and teach your betters, Robert Charles," JT said with his first full laugh in days.

Bobby was up and dusting himself off now, dabbing at the scorch of powder on his cheek, and then he laughed too.

"Bring back memories?" JT asked, tucking his thumbs into his belt loops.

"Too many," Bobby said, spitting out flecks of dirt. He stomped at a couple of embers dropped by the rocket, lest they kindle wildfire and continue the ruination of the day. "Guess we'd better save the rest of these for the green green woods of Coloraddy, or this whole county may go up in…" He stopped grooming and squinted across the golden wasteland. He trotted to a barbed wire fence marking the property line. Pushing himself up with care, he stood on the bottom wire and waved JT over.

JT came, scanning for several seconds before his expression registered what Bobby had noticed. A large patch of green broke the sea of brown and yellow. Several hundred yards farther up the bending road, a single farm stood with proud healthy rows of corn. Drought and rot had left a single virgin oasis in the desert.

"Is that what it looks like? I wish I had Lisa's binocs with me." Bobby put his camera to his eye, but the view through the long lens did not satisfy him.

"I'm no farmer," JT said, "but if I had crops like that, I'd get my butt to work picking them, harvest time or not. That guy's gonna poach the market for miles if his neighbors don't gang up and steal his corn."

"What gives, you think?"

"Hell if I know," said JT. "Guy's got some good seed or scarecrows, or both."

"Huh," Bobby said. He searched the sky above the farm, but at such a distance couldn't tell whether the dark circling specks were genuine birds or imaginary. He thought he heard a frenzy of caws, but with no wind to carry them it might have been a trick of the mind. If what he thought was real, it would seem a whole flock had been stirred up. A murder.

"I just remembered something," JT said. "You'll never guess what that dog's name was."

"What dog?" Bobby was equally engrossed watching the sky.

"What dog do you think, dummy? The old guy called it 'Tompall.' You believe that?"

"Believe it? I don't even understand it. What's a Tompall?"

"Tompall Glaser. He was a singer, ran with the Willie and Waylon crowd but never made it as big."

"You're making this up."

"You don't remember that record of Dad's?" He tried humming a line but couldn't pick the tune up. "Something about logs on the fire. Real corny." He glanced at the acres of land around them, wincing at his own word choice. "Cheesy."

"Ah, hell," Bobby said. "Sure, I remember. Dad thought that shit was hilarious. Wouldn't stop playing it! Who names a dog after that?"

"Only the finest entertainment host in the Cornhusker Land. Tompall must be a Nebraska boy."

"I guess," Bobby said. He squeezed out a dry laugh, but it

died. The atmosphere in that place was wrong for laughter.

"Some field of corn, though," JT said.

Back at the roadside parking spot, Lisa stood in the shade of the camper, scanning for birds with her binoculars. Katy had excused herself for a pee in the weeds.

Although not in the correct line of sight to spot the farm, she identified the circling flecks in the cloudless blue as crows. A dozen or more swirled in a tight loop, almost like a shoal of fish. It was not exactly out of natural order, given their wily and unpredictable nature, but it was unusual. Unless…

"Ah," she breathed as the answer came. A lone vulture, two or three times the size of its fellow birds, veered into their orbit on its own slow circle. She could not doubt something was dead or dying up the road.

The crows banked in what Lisa could only think of as an attack formation. They clawed and pecked at the larger bird, jolting it out of its flight pattern. Lisa gasped. The crows took turns at the weakened vulture until it tumbled from the sky. From that height, it was unlikely to survive the fall. She could see the desperate flutter of a broken wing as it struggled to right itself. Instead of letting it go, four of the aggressor birds latched their talons to a part of its body and hammered it with concentrated blows of their beaks, as if they meant to quarter their prey and pull it apart on the wing. The five-bird mass whirled and undulated like a feathered flying saucer, slowly descending toward the treetops. The crows continued their frenzied pecking as they slipped out of view.

Lisa dropped her binoculars and put one hand to her mouth. "Holy heck," she said in a reverent whisper. She knew crows fought owls, and probably other birds, for territory all the time, but nothing would have prepared her for that sort of display. If Mother Nature had gone bloodthirsty in these parts, it was probably best they made their way somewhere greener by the shortest road possible.

"Oh man," she said, "am I seriously the only one who saw that?"

Katy emerged from the brush.

"Saw what?" she asked.

CHAPTER FIVE

An Elephant's Eye

The brothers waved down the shoulder, gesturing for the women to join them. Katy and Lisa traded looks of curiosity, then jogged up the shoulder together to see what was going on. When Bobby and JT led them down a rough-cut path in the dry weeds, ignoring all questions, new mysteries erased old ones.

"Good grief almighty," said Katy when they all stood before the towering green stalks.

The cornfield was thick as a jungle and a head taller than Bobby. A worn rail fence encompassed the crop, seeming to bulge outward against its barely contained bounty. Judging from the visible side of the property, the farm did not look especially large. Yet, the monstrous crops blocked any view of its general layout. It was as if the wall of corn, not the warped fence, was there to guard the farmer and his people from interlopers and prying eyes.

"Someone call the Four Horsemen," said Bobby, framing a series of shots with his Canon as he paced up and down the fence. "Somebody left a green patch in Nebraska. Can corn even grow this big?"

"Well, it did," said Lisa, staring past him at the looming vegetation.

Katy gave JT a nudge. "It can't be…natural?"

"Hell no," said Bobby. "Got to be dusting it with some top-secret Monsanto compound made of Agent Orange and puppy's teeth."

"You slept through Ag Business, as I recall," said Lisa. "And chemistry."

JT had only a few weekend seminars of agricultural expertise but knew enough to shake his head. More than Mother Nature was at work here. "High summer and this field's ripe as it's gonna get, liable to bust this fence apart. Makes not one dime of sense to me," he said almost in a whisper, sounding uncannily to himself like his own father.

"Probably, we're all going sterile just being this close to it," said Bobby. That got a snort from JT.

Katy wrinkled her face. "Jee-zus, Bobby."

Bobby, pleased with his almost-wit, threw an elbow into Lisa. She gave him a game sneer of appreciation, but the look sank from her face as soon as Bobby looked away. Something about his "going sterile" comment bothered her.

"Come here, Leese," Bobby said, fiddling with his f-stop. "I need you to stand in for scale." Lisa, clearly accustomed to that request, blinked her foggy expression away and shuffled to the fence. She turned to Bobby with a toss of her hair.

"Ohh… Seduce me, mystical corn woman," said Bobby, and crouched for a low-angle shot.

"Don't take those," Lisa said. "Not in my contract. I hate that angle."

"I need to show how high it grows. You're too short for a head-on shot."

"No way. You'll see right up my nose."

"I'm almost done. Quit being a snot. Hey, speaking of which…" He knelt with comic exaggeration to point the camera straight up her nose. "Yeah, that's hot!" he cried. "Gimme some finger action, babe."

Lisa kicked him over. Bobby rocked over on his back with the wounded expression of a flipped turtle, thrusting his camera protectively in the air. That got a laugh from the others.

JT allowed himself another cigarette, turning away as if he could keep Katy from seeing him light up. She kept a tight-lipped gaze fixed on him while he studied bristle-headed corn stalks against the fading sky. It was time to head back and organize camp, but the placid spot had a definite appeal despite its eeriness.

"All the green tells me someone found water in the desert," Bobby said.

The others murmured in agreement.

"Or else it's all a big mirage," he said.

"It's… kinda beautiful, I guess," Lisa said.

"It's nicer to look at than all the nothing out here," said Katy. "But…"

"You don't trust it," JT said, almost to himself. Katy shot him a questioning look, as if he'd either said something totally off base or read her mind verbatim. He didn't look back at her, but slipped his free arm around her shoulders. He held his burning cigarette at arm's length away from her, and they stood that way for a silent minute.

The sun broke their contact. It was not far past its peak brightness of the day. Having left his aviators in the camper, JT released his hold on Katy to shade his eyes. Cold alarm jabbed him.

A shape rested among the cool green textures. It was deep enough in that he could only discern the outline by concentrating, and tall enough that he drew an unsteady breath, ready to alert the others. Then his vision tuned itself to the rough burlap surfaces and spread arms. The thing rustled in a light breeze, but though he could not feel the wind he could see perfectly well that this was a scarecrow, all but overgrown by the crops it stood guarding. The sight was impressive, never mind his nagging sense that they had come to gawk at a sideshow without paying the admission price.

Lisa had grabbed Katy to pose with her, runway-style, before the curtain of green.

"Hey, grab yourselves an ear," said Bobby, caught up in the silliness. "Like a prop. You know, do a *Charlie's Angels* thing."

The girls looked at a fat yellow ear of corn above their

heads, nearly the size of a junior football in its crackling silk jacket.

"Um… nah," Lisa said.

"Come on!" said Bobby.

"I'm not stealing corn," said Katy.

"Stealing? Oh, come on."

"Seriously," Lisa said, "that's just, like, vandalism."

"For the love of… you're fired! Both of you." He stepped forward and grabbed the ear at the stalk and shook it.

"Knock it off!" said Lisa. She laughed as corn silk fell in her hair. Katy stepped away, not laughing.

JT pinched his cigarette out half-smoked. "Bobby, you're a child."

"And you," Bobby said, "are an old green turkey fart." The ear snapped loose in his hand, and he cradled it against his chest. The thing was more like a regulation football up close. "Ho-lee hell, Batman," Bobby said, hefting it from hand to hand. "Mutant miracle corn."

Lisa tried to swat it away from him. "Come on, moron. Leave it here and let's—"

The cornfield gave a violent rustle, and something inside it let off a watery croak. Four pairs of feet left the ground. Both women shrieked. Something black and feathery hopped onto the lower fence rail, beating its wings. It scolded them again, sounding more like an angry old woman than a bird.

"Fuck me," said Bobby.

"Yeah," said JT as he drew in breath, "fuck you, Bobby."

More crows emerged from the corn, about a dozen in all. It seemed absurd for adult people to inch backward like in some dumb cartoon, but they did so. The birds had not flown down from overhead. They had crawled out from among the rows of corn. Rather than the sleek specimens painted or photographed for field guides, these crows were sluggish and misshapen.

Several continued advancing along the ground, as fearless as yard geese. They did not caw but made a kind of strangled rasp that sounded even less friendly. Despite her alarm, Lisa could not resist crouching down to study one that stood before her pointing its beak her way.

"This is, like, next level weird," she said. "Bobby, can these crows even fly, do you think?"

Bobby shrugged. "Fat as a damn bucket of ticks," he said.

Even the two or three birds that sat on the lower fence wire looked precarious and ready to topple. Two of the grounded birds came waddling over to where Bobby had dropped the massive ear of corn. Grasping with their beaks, they took turns dragging and rolling it away, back to their turf.

"Well, I'll be dipped in dog poop," said Bobby. He took half a step forward and both birds turned on him with savage cries of reproach. Bobby retreated. "Most unbelievable thing I ever saw."

"Guess he'll want his money back on the scarecrows," JT said.

"Lisa, Katy!" Bobby cried. "Hunker down and pose with the birdies."

"Nope," said Katy, who looked cold despite the weather. "No way, Bobby. I'm done."

"Yeah, bro," said JT. "Enough's enough. Session's wrapped."

"The hell it is," said Bobby. "I'm gonna send these shots to magazines!"

"Yeah, well American Shitbird Illustrated will have to wait 'til the next time you pass this way. Let's get that tire off and changed while the women fix dinner."

"Excuse me?" Katy hollered.

"Okay," JT said, "you win. I'll cook and you girls change the damned thing."

Lisa slugged his arm.

"Listen," Bobby said, "I'll change the tire myself and sing you a pretty song while I do it, if you give me just one group shot."

It took some close huddling, but Bobby composed a low-angle frame that would include all four of them, the fence, the wall of corn, and a few of the waddling birds between their feet. The camera sat on the ground, propped on a desiccated cob he had found outside the fence, and he set the timer for a short series of auto-exposures. Even JT seemed impressed by Bobby's quick mastery of the digital interface. JT typically slouched away from photos, as if in genuine fear of having his soul stolen and uploaded to sinister access grids.

Bobby scampered into place and threw his hands up, cocking spindly fingers into a set of heavy metal horns. Comically uncool and proud of it. "It'll take a few," he said through his teeth. "Everyone hold still a minute."

A reedy gurgle at his elbow made him flinch. Before he could turn to look, a crow hopped its way to the upper fence wire between the brothers. It pushed itself against his shoulder, big and warm as a feathered cat, then turned its attention to JT.

JT asked Bobby, obviously trying to ignore it, "Could you get that sad old scarecrow in frame back there?"

"Ah, hell! You didn't tell me there was—"

JT cut his brother off with a yelp. Wiggling its puny wings, the crow had jumped onto his shoulder, clawing once or twice for purchase. JT flinched away, but Katy gripped the back of his shirt.

"Damn it all," he spat. "It's on me now."

"Smile," Katy said, enjoying a little revenge. The camera started beeping off exposures.

"It'll look great!" Bobby hissed. "Don't scare it away."

Between the second and third photo, JT roared in pained surprise, pulling loose from the group pose. Katy screamed.

Lisa made sounds of amazement.

The crow had clamped its beak onto the meat of his ear and seemed determined to pull it loose. Its talons gripped his shirt and the flesh beneath, so it could alternate between chewing his ear and pecking at the hairline. JT danced in grotesque circles, tearing at the oily feathers that beat against his cheek. Hot blood oozed from his broken scalp down the right side of his head.

Bobby, speechless for once, caught JT in a bear hug as if he was the unruly party. Katy lunged for the bird with both hands, pulled it off her husband along with tiny tufts of his hair and skin for souvenirs, and pitched it into the wispy tangle of green and gold from which it had come. Then she turned to JT, transformed to her caring self again after defending her mate, all matters of petty spite forgotten.

JT had a look in his eye that visibly upset her. He looked ready to jump the fence and start stomping anything too slow to get away. Instead, he shook off Bobby's grip, turning on his heels and heading toward the path to the camper.

"JT," Katy said.

"When that spare is on," JT said without stopping, in a tone they could not mistake, "this bus rolls. All aboard, or God help your sorry butts." End of transmission. The captain had spoken. Bobby remarked, only to himself, how like their father JT walked when he was angry.

Katy stood collecting herself, taking long meditative breaths through her nose, eyes shut.

"So," Lisa ventured, "field trip's over?"

Bobby scratched his thumbnail over a drop of blood on his shirt. Katy was examining one on her shorts.

"Just when the light's getting perfect," Bobby mumbled.

"Stay here and finish up, then," Katy said with perfect calm. "Let me go talk him down. You take your time."

She rested a kind hand on his shoulder, then strolled off the way JT had gone.

Bobby blinked at Lisa, fingering the outer casing of his camera lens. "Does she actually want us to go with her, or stay here? I can never tell which one girls mean."

Lisa put her arms around his broad chest. "Oh, Bobby," she said sweetly enough but with a shake of her head. He relaxed in her embrace and kissed her.

"I say we let them be for a little bit," Lisa said. "He might leave us here, but she won't. Be nice for everybody to have some alone time, together."

They kissed more, relaxing into each other until the time came to look for a more sheltered spot. She sighed through parted lips, and he responded in kind.

Bobby opened his eyes. The light had changed. The spell was broken, the eerie isolation of the spot intruding on them. They were not about to do it in the weeds while a flock of malformed crows looked on. Though, if he had asked, she might have said yes. Nothing to lose but a little comfort and dignity, which had no real place in sex and were easily found again later.

Something else took Bobby's mind away too. It was golden hour, and Lisa knew him well enough to understand that the chance for a few more shots in that perfect light made him almost as hard as the gentle press of her hips.

He pulled away gingerly, anxious not to offend her with his eager shift of attention. She released him with a smile he recognized as generous.

"Not really the spot for romance," she said. "But you'll owe me. Go make art."

He surged with a boyish, almost canine feeling of loving devotion.

"Okay," he said, "but you're coming with me." And he bounded to the fence to swing his leg up.

"Wait a minute!" she said, but he was over in a flash,

parting the corn like a safari guide.

"You better come on back."

"Come on, Leese. Make way before the sun burns out."

"That's not a saying!" she called.

"Of course it is. I said it."

"Get back here," she said. "Crossing fences is a different deal. People get shot that way!"

"I'm just going a few yards in," he said, not stopping. "If someone hollers at me, I'll make like Mr. Straw Man here. Hot damn, look at that ugly thing! Hop on over quick, Lisa. Don't catch your overalls."

"Bobby, it's not a good idea," she said, already muffled through the weird foliage between them. "Remember JT?"

"You're too sweet for any mean birds to attack," he said. "And I'll protect you if they do."

He'd lost all sense of the growing distance between them, and would have turned back if he hadn't heard a rustle of movement near the fence that, in his mind, indicated that she'd decided to follow after all. He gave into giddiness and kept tramping, certain she could follow his trail. They might have lucked into a sexy little game of chase after all. With the bizarro gang of birds left behind them to snack on corn, the only other figures in the waning light were scarecrows, and scarecrows weren't likely to notice much.

CHAPTER SIX

Down on the Farm

The work brought a calming focus to JT. In the main storage well, he found a brand-new spare and a fully-packed road safety kit, heavy work gloves included. Underneath lay a sturdy hydraulic pump jack, the bottle-shaped kind his old man had called a "whiskey jack." He suspected that the camper's owner had changed a lot of tires in rotten weather or dangerous conditions. The equipment was all new and looked expensive, the sign of a motorist who intended never to be caught with cheap or inadequate tools for any problem that might hobble his multi-ton rolling refuge.

He had allowed Katy to dress his ear and face, burning the wounds clean with alcohol and taping gauze into the bigger gashes. He mumbled conciliatory words of thanks and planted a soft kiss on her forehead. While he worked with the jack, she opened beers and found snacks for them, singing softly as she did so. Usually, it mortified her to sing in front of others, but she had a good voice and he liked it when she did.

Despite his supreme irritation at being scaled by an upstart crow, JT had exercised a measure of restraint for once. He'd wanted to throw a punch, first at his brother and then through a window of the camper. Katy had sensed it, he knew. She must have dreaded the increasing likelihood of a knockdown brotherly confrontation, precisely because she did not bring it up. They chatted about any old foolish thing but their present frustrations. No lug nuts went missing in the grass. No fingers got crushed. It was the first thing to go right all day, besides the dubious mercy of a lone state trooper. As the new tire touched ground and took the weight from the lowered jack, JT sighed with something like amazement.

There were more surprises waiting. Katy, who had vanished into the dark stillness of the camper some time earlier, leaned out at him. "Before you get too cooled off," she said, "I found one more thing that needs fixing in here."

JT tensed, his thrill at completing a big chore interrupted. He did not fully consider the remark or register that her shorts no longer peeked from beneath the fishing shirt. Only when he stepped into the camper, suppressing a grumble, and saw she had abandoned the shirt as well, did he understand.

She did not give him a chance to rinse off. She added his dust and sweat to her own. Free of distractions in the solitude of the camper, JT and Katy found each other again. Sex with her had always been easy for him, more natural and less inhibited than with previous partners. The stress of hard travel, including the residue of their latest argument, added enthusiasm to the lovemaking and promised a sweeter payoff. While he knew she took no pleasure in the act of bickering, he believed she came most often and most passionately during a reconciliation. He loved her secret wildness in those moments, because it was something they kept between the two of them. It worked a strange magic on him too, coaxing tender whispers from him against the grain of his tough, taciturn demeanor.

This encounter proved as rich as ever. His anxiety receded as he slowed his pace to prolong their contact, while she uttered beautiful profane sounds against his neck that she would never have dared in daylight.

Lisa could not understand how Bobby had moved out of earshot so quickly. Her slow progress through the corn, after finally climbing the fence, must have made as much noise as a rhinoceros. She didn't think corn was supposed to grow, as it did here, with fat vines creeping between the rows to draw the stalks into haphazard webs and snarls.

"Bobby!" she called. "Damn it, Bobby. Where did you go?" Her irritation was turning to anger, a natural defense mechanism to mask her overriding fear. A dreadful vision of being caught and held by green tendrils dragged at her imagination. She sensed their clinging menace, the way it must worry a fly to realize it's blundered near the center of a large web.

Bobby should have been able to hear her calling, even if he had charged ahead through the corn, but new adventures tended to draw his focus down to a tiny point and drown out the wider world. Instead of breaking an ankle trying to overtake him, she decided to make her way back to where they had crossed the fence and wait. Once he had run in a few excited circles and gotten some pictures, he would have sense enough to return there, assuming they could both find the spot again.

She thought of the scarecrow, which she had only perceived as a vague shape, but should make a good landmark. She found traces of her own path in the corn, but fewer and fewer as she doubled back. It almost seemed as if the corn was growing before her eyes to fill in the gaps made by the young trespassers. Nonetheless, she followed her instinct and soon saw a gap ahead, where the corn ended and the open sky began.

Bobby was a few hundred feet along when he realized Lisa was not gaining on him. Creeping through the gnarls of corn with excitement filling his belly, he had possibly mistaken another noise for her climbing the fence to catch up. Guilt poked him now. It was not the first time he had run off in the thrill of adventure.

He stopped to look and listen.

"Leese?" he called. "Lisa?" His voice was tentative, not the search-party bellow he should have used, because something in the sudden quiet of the cornfield made him self-conscious. A sudden profound sense of isolation overwhelmed him, but also the strong possibility that they could be easily observed without knowing it. How had he convinced himself otherwise a few minutes before? He shuddered and would have turned back right away if not for spotting the full sky breaking through the edge of the field, the sun like a fire consuming the entire western horizon. Bobby was conscious of the hypnotic influence the stunning view worked on him but let it draw him forward anyway.

A barn towered against the sunset, vast and stately as a fortress in its humble rural setting. Bobby fluttered his eyes, adjusting them to the contrast of black shadow and brilliant orange. A group of shabby-looking figures, maybe half a dozen farmhands, were gathered at a large door loading heavy bundles of something inside. Bobby could not have asked for a better book-jacket photo, perhaps for some gloomy classic novel about the Dust Bowl.

Promising himself to get serious and find Lisa after one more perfect shot, he hunkered down on his belly to work undetected, fiddling with his aperture to capture the very best of pure, corn-fed Americana.

Lisa kicked at green creepers like swollen fingers, which kept snagging her by the shoes and working the knots of her laces free. Right where she expected, a stout wooden post appeared in her path. Driven deep into the earth, it was sturdy to the touch despite its weathered appearance. Lisa entertained a mental picture of corn roots gripping it on all sides, holding the heavy wood steady, fixed forever in place. But she had made a mistake.

The post was bare, no scarecrow hung upon it. Her forward brain accepted without argument that the uneven lacework of corn had disoriented her, putting her on a false heading. Her lower brain, the intuitive parts tuned into danger, told her something different. It would be best to get across the fence and off the strange property as soon as she could.

Lisa only realized how quiet the cornfield had gone at sundown when a chorus of squawks and shrieks rose before her, accompanied by a flapping, undulating tide of black that occluded her view of safety. Despite dozens of crippled and malformed birds now squirming past her ankles like feathered rats, an equal number of them could still fly. They bounced off her shoulders, clawed feet scratching the bare arms she put up to protect her face, as they swirled upward in a cyclone of frenzy.

By the time the curtain of birds lifted from her line of sight, the thing that had spooked them was close. Lisa's reason denied what she saw. Her mind could not equate the shape bearing down on her with the missing figure from the empty post, but the evidence before her eyes was reason enough to go and go quickly. The tattered form of her pursuer was roughly man-sized, moving on two legs with one sleeve hanging empty and one powerful arm lifted toward her.

Lisa made an impressive leap in the opposite direction, kicking the shoe clean off her right foot. She landed in a full sprint, charging through the corn heedless of the pummels and scratches it dealt her as she went. The angry crows were loud enough to hurt her ears. She would never have expected that the aerial attack she had witnessed before might be a premonition. She was not sure whether to be more afraid of the thing shambling at her heels or the fury of combative birds. More than once, her shoeless foot had fallen on a mass of delicate bird bones that crunched beneath her weight, blood and sticky gobbets of meat accumulating on her sock as the crawling bird gave a strangled death-cry. She did not stop to take stock of the carnage underfoot.

A familiar voice called to Lisa as she broke from the corn into open ground, but she did not register the sound until the field and its lurking horrors were far behind her. As temporary sunset blindness receded, a large barn towered to her right. Slowing her pace, she found herself moving across an empty farmyard.

Bobby had nearly leapt out of his skin when Lisa came tearing through the corn at him, jumping over his prone body like an antelope on fire.

"Lisa!" he cried hoarsely after her, unable to fill his lungs properly in his awkward position. "Holy crap."

He had been prepared for humble apologies, fearing that to lose track of him in the knotted crops might freak her out. However, he had not anticipated any danger great enough to put her in a panic. Lisa was not the type. It would have taken something beyond reasonable cornfield claustrophobia to trigger such a full-on flight response. Something had to have chased her.

A good distance back the way Lisa had come, Bobby saw and heard a whirl of agitated crows in the sky. They dove mostly one at a time, occasionally in twos, from the larger cluster, the attack swarm, concentrating their aggression on something in the corn Bobby could not see. No voice cried out, human or otherwise. He heard only the terror and blood-frenzy of crows.

Lisa was already out of sight against the vanishing sun.

Whatever had set her running, friend or foe, crazy birds or something he hadn't encountered, did not matter. He wasted no more time getting on his feet and moving across the open farmland in search of her.

Lisa's heart, still beating at a dangerous pace, allowed her raw senses to take in only the basic visual details of the yard. To her left, she saw a cluster of pens meant for pigs and other small livestock. Whether they had rotted or been broken open was a mystery, but not even one stood intact. Beyond the pens was a low structure, once a henhouse but long since devastated. A downy strew of soot-black feathers adorned the roof, stuck fast by dried patches of greenish bird droppings and something else that was rusty brown. Lisa made a quick guess about what might have attacked the hens long ago. The side of the coop toward the house was blackened and partly burned away, perhaps in an attempt to repel the predatory pest birds.

The farmhouse was the main feature, quaint but badly dilapidated. The white siding appeared green and black with moldy patches. Any trace of window glass was long gone, replaced by uneven slats and nailed up to keep the elements out. The porch and outer walls canted at unsafe angles, and the roof looked ready to slide off if someone hit it just right with a pinecone, or a big ear of corn.

An antique farm pickup, slatted wood sides and all, rested on blocks a short distance from the porch. Lisa got close enough to see that nobody was in it, and obviously nobody had driven it for a while.

She proceeded toward the house, observing a pile of scrap lumber and other detritus that partially blocked access to the front door.

"Shit, Bobby," she said to herself. "Only you would want pictures of whatever's in there."

This declaration did not stop her from beginning an immediate search for the best way in.

Bobby had lost track of Lisa in the descending sun's glare. Furthermore, he saw no sign of the hired hands whose activity had drawn his attention to the barn in the first place. It was a hell of a relic, a symbol of a bygone age, shored up here and there with inexpert props and patches. Whoever kept it standing had not possessed the brainpower or been paid wages enough to restore it properly, but some of its old heartland glory shone through.

Near the peak of the roof was a small window to ventilate the loft. Normally it would be wide enough to allow the passage of hay and other goods through it, but a tangle of sharp wire and detritus covered the dark opening.

The barn was clearly off limits to crows. Above the window hung three bird bodies by nails driven through their decomposing ribcages, their wings pulled to full spread like emblems from the battle flags of fallen tyrants. It was quite a response to an airborne pest population, staged with maximum aggression. Bobby would have liked to pause for close-ups of those details and more, but the urgency of catching up with Lisa had cured his attack of shutterbug fever.

In her place, Bobby might have taken the chance to lie low and explore the barn. But the house and yard a short distance away were more likely Lisa's first choice for refuge. He was all set to look there first and double back if needed, He whistled softly, a sound she would recognize, and listened hard for a reply. A faint voice emanated from inside the barn. It was shrill and oddly rhythmic, like a song.

He could not easily picture it being Lisa, but it had sounded human. If someone was in the barn, they might have talked to Lisa or know where to look for her. Bobby gathered his good ol' boy manners to greet the barn's occupant. He would apologize for the intrusion and offer a handshake of goodwill. Be neighborly, be dealt with neighborly, his mother had said.

The crooked barn door was unsettlingly quiet as he eased open a big enough gap to squeeze inside. He went carefully, not intending to surprise anyone before his charm could work. The interior of the barn seemed wider than it had appeared from outside. At the far end sat rusty piles of material, discarded hulks of combine equipment, and possibly some antiquated pumping system. He could not tell for sure. The high, aimless tune persisted, and he followed it to three sagging wooden pens against the wall, for keeping stock in out of the weather.

The first two appeared to have been deserted for some time. A hay fork and a pair of broken lanterns were the only furnishings. Creeping over to the third pen, he found the owner of the curious voice—a woman, hunched with age or very hard-used, perched on an old-fashioned milking stool. Her head rested against the side of a peculiar creature, her withered hand stroking its flank as she sang.

Bobby took a sharp breath into his nose as his vision adjusted to the lightless corner. Never mind that the woman sat milking without a lantern. Farm folks rose before the sun and probably did chores that way all the time. What troubled him was the animal, which was not the typical leather, hair, and hoof specimen. It seemed to be an imitation of a cow, an effigy close to life size, propped up on sawhorse legs. The bulk of the body was straw and corn husks baled together. In the span of one late afternoon, Bobby had gotten his fill of corn, and the dry rustle of the dummy cow made him uneasy.

What truly flipped his stomach was the profusion of cow bones peeking through the stuffing, lashed into an approximation of their living structure. The disagreeable likeness had been built on the framework of an old cow skeleton. The fact that it could give no milk did not seem to trouble the woman engaged in soothing it.

She seemed to sense him there, despite his silence and the fact that she could not possibly see him. Bobby almost ran when she turned her head enough to reveal her collapsed profile, but her eyes were lifted toward the ceiling as if in prayer. Her peripheral vision did not appear to pick him up, yet the beat-up kitchen knife she held against her cow's haunch made him think twice about sudden moves. He judged it best to let her leave the barn first if he could.

Dropping slowly to his knees, then to his belly, he rolled around the side of a junk heap, the only one not full of sharp edges and rust. It was softer, mostly hay and castoff clothes, denim legs and flannel sleeves stuffed and half-stuffed in a creepy jumble. This was a scrap pile for building scarecrows. The appetites of those massive birds outside the barn must have kept the scarecrow-makers busy, but something told him there must be more to the story than could be seen in the cornfield. He watched the woman sway on her stool, either reaching the peak of her singing or preparing to topple over onto the dirt. Nothing would surprise him.

He was wrong. When the pile of straw limbs began to writhe around him, he howled with fright. Dirty gloved hands pulled at his face. Powerful limbs, hidden under flimsy rustic trappings, gripped him at the joints. He flailed against them but could barely move. Of the six figures that had untangled themselves from the pile, none had more than ordinary strength, but they worked together to hold him. The ugly stitched faces of scarecrows gaped a dozen eyeless sockets at him.

With a jerk that almost dislocated his shoulder, Bobby freed his arm and shoved one assailant back. He drove two fingers into hollow eyeholes, shivering at the firm spongy tissue they found to hook into, and yanked downward with all his might. The scarecrow made a deep bow and swayed upright again. Only its head continued backward on the broken axis of neck, flopping useless between the creature's shoulders before the body crashed to the ground.

A stunning blow took the starch out of Bobby. Another scarecrow had smashed one of the old lanterns against the crown of his head. His vision blurred and turned a strange color for several seconds. One eye came back to normal, but a film of red had fallen over the other.

The old woman stood before him, unconcerned by the living horrors around her. Head-on she was a far greater shock than from the side. Her complexion, pocked with sores and cancerous-looking growths, looked scarcely more human than the monsters restraining his limbs.

She stretched out cracked fingers that looked to have healed badly from an ancient fracture, examining the camera still hanging at Bobby's neck. He opened his mouth to protest, and spit dribbled from his bottom lip. She no longer formed syllables but continued to issue a steady sound from her stinking maw, a soft insistent "e-e-ehhh…"

The knife rose to his face, lifting a corner of his lip on its point. The pain was duller than he'd expected, but warm blood washed his teeth as she examined them like an auction bidder. He could not restrain a high-pitched whine of his own, which she answered by modulating her voice to a strained, "eeeeeeEEEEEE…"

Long swaths of linen and burlap circled his body. The scarecrows bound him like a mold-blackened mummy with alarming speed. He thrashed wormlike against it. Then he was moving, borne on spindly shoulders across the barn to where planks had been nailed in a crude ladder to the loft above. They shoved him upward, mindless of how his head crashed against the wood. Bobby's final glimpse of the ground was the crazy old woman, already paying him no mind once he was gone from her sight. She squatted in the dirt, poking something with her knife. It was his camera, which had slid off him in the scuffle.

His bad eye was nearly gummed shut with blood. Three more sack-heads appeared in the opening above and hauled him up by the feet while he called Lisa's name with all the voice he had left.

The porch wood buckled beneath Lisa's feet, threatening to splinter and trap her leg in a jagged hole for the enjoyment of any creepy crawlies living under the house. If the insects here were anything like the birds, Lisa didn't want to imagine them. She slid her feet across the boards, putting as little weight down as possible. She found the door without a knob or handle, but a light push was sufficient to shift the overturned chair bracing it shut.

She expected a cozy country kitchen, or at least the mummified remains of one, with a cupboard or some space large enough to hide her until she could form an escape plan. She needed to know who or what else might be prowling the grounds. To her surprise, she dropped from the threshold to a packed earthen floor, well-trodden but bare of coverings. She scanned the dim interior, confirming that it was almost completely empty. Small piles of crumbling matter, old cornsilk mostly, littered the dirt. She moved with care, holding both hands out before her until a feeling of heat stopped her short.

The antique wood stove, compact and almost invisible against other dark surfaces, came close to searing the flesh off Lisa's palm. It gave off acrid wisps of smoldering fibrous matter, but no light to speak of. It was the source of the room's overriding funk, sharp like black toast or scorched paper towels or burning… Popcorn, she realized without having to search her mind very hard.

A cooking pot sat on the tiny flat cooking surface, belching a rank smell from within. Peering down, she saw that the vessel was rimmed with fuzzy matter, brimming with more cornsilk and half-chewed cobs, boiled and re-boiled in the same rancid water to an astounding level of rot and fermentation.

It seemed unlikely that any occupant of the house had been able to survive long in such conditions. As Lisa reconsidered taking her chances in the yard again, perhaps after prying loose a window slat to use for a weapon, a narrow door swung out from the wall. She could not suppress a yip of dismay.

A small wiry man, hunched with poor health or age or both, stood bathed in feeble orange light. Some sort of candle or improvised lamp glowed in his left hand. He stepped into the dirt room with a lopsided, spidery gait. His joints made papery sounds as he moved, and he smelled none too clean. Even in the dim illumination, she could see what looked like sores on his face. A stiff rootlike arm held the light not before him but out to one side. He likely needed it to see her, but he kept his face turned from it, as though it hurt him to look directly at the small fire.

Horrified fascination had planted Lisa to the spot, silent and open-mouthed. But the crash of something outside being overturned flipped her "on" switch once more. She wanted the sound to be Bobby, all of it somehow a big joke, but she did not dare hope.

"Listen," she said, "I'm…sorry to be here." That was true in every sense. "I got separated from…from my friend in…the corn." She'd left the door open, an admission that she had been trespassing despite whatever medieval measures might be used to punish such an act in these parts. Her mind abuzz with confusion, her eyes darted across every dark corner in search of Bobby.

The farmer gave a chortle—not with any true humor, but the sort of thing people did when trying to sound pleasant. Above his rumpled, tooth-poor grin, his eyes widened with what might have been dreadful amazement at seeing another human.

"Listen," she said, "we were taking pictures on your fence, and I think Bobby…my friend, got lost around here. He might have made some of the birds mad. You have some… big ones around here. If I could maybe use your telephone…"

The absurdity of the request hit Lisa when the man laughed out loud. It was a harsh ugly sound, as though he had not practiced it in decades, but unmistakable in its unhinged glee.

"No phones, little sister. Man from the county ain't been out lately!" He tittered like a silly girl, calculating how best to express amusement and friendliness.

Lisa suppressed a burp of nausea at the blackness of his devastated gums. Although speaking in her direction, he did not appear to be addressing her but someone else in the room. That made Lisa's mind up.

"I'd better get going," she said. "Sorry to be a bother." She strangled the tremor out of her voice, moving back the way she had come without taking her eyes off him.

He made no move to restrain her, but motioned toward the stove and the putrid stew pot instead. "Plenty of supper on for all."

"No, thanks." Lisa groped behind her for the door but had not gone far enough backward. If she stumbled and fell to the ground, she would be done for.

The farmer ignored her. "Once you've ate you can set a spell while I hunt up that feller of yours. Time was, young folks was always getting lost in our fields," the farmer said with a close mimicry of fondness. "Chasing and foolish catching, young love games. We never held it agin' them. Only jumping fences can be powerful dangerous, and young folks never did have no respect."

His face twitched in momentary wrath, as if transforming into an entirely new person. Had he lurched a step in her direction? Lisa could not be certain.

"Even so," he continued, his benign face restored, "we never met a one we didn't ask in for supper."

Lisa resolved to get away, and take her chances running into the sunset, without having to find out what the word "we" was supposed to mean. Whatever had run at her in the cornfield was the more straightforward threat. She knew her slasher lore well enough to picture a lunatic farm hand or the farmer's disfigured son lurking among the corn, scaring strangers to get his inbred rocks off.

She reached behind her, probing the door's empty knob-hole, until a sudden force jolted her around. An old woman, or possibly a living pile of dirty laundry topped with a cheap wig, waddled in through the doorway, taking little if any notice of Lisa. A pitted carving knife danced in her hand, swaying in time with her skulking rhythm, conducting unheard music.

Lisa jumped back from the waving blade, shielding her chest with folded arms. The woman's pitiful gums worked violently, as if still chewing whatever had made off with her teeth. Her throat issued a continuous chorus of soft, mousy gibberish. A black, irregular box of something dangled from a strap around her neck. She glared at random spots around the room, evidently blind or close to it, searching for shapes and spots of light of which there were none worth mentioning.

Her *husband? brother? son?* piped up as she passed. "We've got a supper guest."

She grasped him with her free hand, the desperate relief of a drowning soul finding a raft, the compassion of domestic harmony in a wasted nest of darkness. She approached the stove and gave the pot a stir, fishing out a ladleful of moldy cob sludge. Rot smell filled the room with renewed force, a stagnant pond disturbed by a careless hand.

"Hours to spend," she rasped, her voice not unlike a crow's. "Time enough to visit."

Lisa planned to make that her exit cue, and would have slipped away beneath the limited awareness of her hosts if a chance glint of the farmer's light off a polished surface hadn't caught her eye. The object around the woman's neck was not some rustic curiosity. It was a high-end camera, and she knew whose.

"Where did you get that?" she asked, advancing to the center of the floor. "That's Bobby's. How come you have it?"

"Ain't no Bobby here," the farmer grumbled. "That's only m'good wife."

Lisa ignored him, stepping up into the milky-eyed face. The woman flinched, hissing in fear through her teeth. She moaned in her husband's direction, her jaw having apparently locked up on her.

"Where the fuck is Bobby, you frazzled hag?"

"No call for it," said the farmer, shuffling impotently. "You're a guest here. No call and no business of your'n." He eyed the window, then the doorway, all anxiety.

Lisa had forgotten her caution, determined to extract answers.

The old woman flailed the sopping ladle in her direction, either a peace offering of food or a myopic swipe of self-defense. Lisa batted the spoon aside, just before the dirty blade slashed her opposite forearm. The knife didn't cut deeply, but drew a scream of rage. With a twirl of her wrist, Lisa wrenched the weapon away, feeling at least one of the madwoman's brittle fingers crack. She jerked the other fragile wrist and pulled. The farmer's wife tumbled to the floor, a mewling heap of old bones in her frayed, filthy clothing. The camera tumbled away into a corner; the strap had broken in the scuffle.

The farmer rushed over, as nimbly as he could, and crouched protectively against his fallen mate.

Lisa advanced, knife extended, not caring how pitiful they looked in her able-bodied clutches. "One of you shitnecks better start talking," she said through her teeth. "Fast. Yes, we trespassed, and that's our fault. But we didn't come to hurt anything, and we were planning to go away quietly when something came at us—"

Those were her last intelligible words as a veil of black dropped over her straining vision. Oily burlap encased her head, its musty smell and taste filling her lungs, the rough weave grating her skin. Lisa whipped her neck from side to side, but to no avail. She had time to hope it was Bobby, that this was all the punchline to some sick prank taken too far, before a hand twisted the sack tight and slammed her head against the stove hard enough to put her lights out.

The ghastly workers on the barn floor hoisted the interloper with the firm skull and breakable neck. Bobby saw twisted legs crammed into toeless boots on all sides of him, and then his captors dropped him to the buckling floor straight on his face.

He curled as small as he could manage, while busy scarecrows went skittering about their hive-chores. One stood sentry over him while another slid a heavy slopping bucket across the planks, and a third reached into a mildewy corn crib. It drew forth a massive ear freshly harvested from the field. Bobby wished for an orgy of gluttonous crows to arrive, to devour the horrible thing before it could touch him. He whispered aimless prayers as the scarecrow dipped the corn, husk and all, into the viscous black contents of the bucket.

The three scarecrows closed on him, solemn in their silence. One knelt on his heaving chest and another pried his broken lips apart. Bobby had time to scream through a mouthful of blood before the third filled him with the bounty of the harvest, body and soul.

CHAPTER SEVEN

Walking After Midnight

JT awoke disoriented. The cramped bunk, the thin rumpled bedding, and the week-old odor of road sweat might have signified one of a dozen road trips from his younger fitter days. Only the ache of his bones, his true age creeping back into his consciousness, told a different story.

He had dreamed an amalgam of busted roadside campouts from the one short tour he ever made as a musician. The venues had mostly been hill country shitkicker dives, full of angry young men he sometimes resented but had certainly understood as kindred souls. The weed had been inexcusably poor, but as plentiful in the wilderness as bread from Heaven.

The smell of Katy recalled him to the present. She was not there, but the bed was warm beside him. She was near.

He barely noticed the dark, because he did not need light to fish the half-smoked cigarette from the pocket of his shirt where it lay on the floor. His fingers went straight to it, programmed by smoker's intuition. He produced his lighter, rolled onto his back and sparked the flint. No sooner did he smell burning tobacco than a thin-fingered hand snaked forward and pulled the lighter from his grip.

JT had thought he was alone, but Katy had returned from wherever she had gone— taking a leak, he guessed—and sat watching him. She clasped her hands around the lighter, hiding it from view against her bare stomach. Her expression was impossible to read without more light, possibly annoyed with him but not without a hint of mischievous triumph.

JT grunted, snatching for the lighter. "Give that back, woman."

She shook her head. Mischief.

"Please," he said.

"Smoke or screw," she said. "You don't get both, and one

you have to do outside."

That got JT's attention. It was a strong remark coming from Katy. She didn't have the same capacity for jagged wit as a lot of JT's friends, but she saved her ammunition for the proper moment. He considered that she might mean it as flirtation, possibly with another tumble in mind. But when she stood up, he could see she had pulled her shorts back on. He had a notion to tempt her back to bed anyway, but rather than push his luck he lay silent and enjoyed the contours of her bare breasts in the dark.

She tucked his lighter into a pocket. He made a playful snatch for it, and she smacked his knuckles, hard.

"One's enough," she said.

"Half."

"Even better," she said, and slipped the pack from the pocket of the pants he'd thrown across the opposite bunk. He heard the last lonely survivor rattle in its coffin. If she crushed it, that would have made him mad, but he allowed her to stow it in the footlocker.

"Tomorrow, you'll want one worse than you do now," she said, "and you'll be a nightmare without it."

"Fine. How about a beer?"

"That'd be nice, thanks."

"I mean, get me one." Then added, "Please." Then added, "Now."

She vanished, and he thought he would have to get one for himself. Then a cold can plopped onto the middle of his chest. He cracked it, sucking up as much foam as he could to minimize any spillage on the floor. It was easy to forget, after so much time, that they did not own the camper.

After he'd sipped off the head and the cheap pilsner ran clean, Katy grabbed it from him and took a long sip before handing it back. He tried to press the can against the small of her back, but she dodged. Too predictable, the old cold-can.

By thunder, he really was turning into his old man.

He said, "You're getting to be a bigger smartass than Lisa. Maybe even Bobby."

She sat on the bed and put her arms through her t-shirt sleeves. Her bra, damp from a long hot day, lay abandoned on the floor. She made a noncommittal sound.

"What's up?" he said, getting a last good puff off the cigarette.

"Lisa," she said. "Well, Bobby too."

"What about them? Is looking after those two knuckleheads putting you in a maternal mood? Don't worry. If my baby brother ever learns to think two minutes ahead into the future, he'll be able to take good care of them both."

The sad look on Katy's face made JT think his careless talk had gone too far. Despite her vulnerable sensibility on some topics, Katy was usually matter of fact about their fitful, so far frustrating, attempts to conceive. A fair amount of medical consultation had confirmed their slim chances. But as far as JT understood, they had decided to leave it to fate. With grim good humor, they found laughing about it sometimes eased the disappointment. The quality of their intimacy had not suffered, when they made the time.

He grasped her hand. "Hell, Katy. I'm sorry, that was—"

She shook her head, but still looked tearful. "No, that's just us being us. I'm not thinking about me."

JT rewound the conversation to review for other thoughtless remarks. She was sensitive about her late father, whose slow dance with terminal cancer made up most of her resolve against JT's smoking habit. But that, too, was a topic they kept light, except during extreme marital arguments. He arrived back at the maternity comment, and it clicked with other points of the trip, unusual reactions and behaviors.

"Lisa?" he asked. "And Bobby?"

She kept her eyes on him, said nothing.

"Are you sure?"

She twitched her head sideways, once, then back to him. "Not, like, medically. And she's acting pretty casual. Don't ask me how, but I'm pretty sure."

"Can I ask how sure you are?"

She shrugged. "Pretty."

"Has she, ah… Does Bobby know?"

Katy laughed, not without humor but not with much joy either. "I'd let her bring it up first."

JT nodded. He realized the cigarette stub was still between his teeth. Swallowing the last of the beer, he ground the butt on the lip of the can and pushed it inside. He wondered whether this was the bombshell that was bound to change the tone of their trip. He wished he could un-hear the news until they were on the way home. But better that he process it now, and avoid all mention once Bobby and Lisa returned from the cornfield.

"Wait a minute," JT said. "What the fuck time is it?"

There was no cattle guard or working gate on the side of the property where they'd posed for Bobby's group photo, but JT located a gap where several posts had toppled. He jumped out and cleared debris to make the opening wide enough for the camper's front end. When he jumped in and started easing forward, Katy grabbed his arm.

"JT" she said, "it's all grown over in front of you."

"I'm not driving into the corn," said JT.

"It sure as hell looks like you are!"

"I'm nosing in a little bit to shine the brights as far into this crap as I can," said JT. "My dumbass brother probably can't find his way back to where he jumped the fence. Happened all the time when we used to hunt with Dad." He hoped the credible detail would hide the tremor of worry in his voice.

"Okay," said Katy. "I've heard property owners like you to use the main gate, especially when they don't know you."

"We're not here to rustle cattle or cut crop circles. I didn't even break the fence. I cleared a couple of fallen posts."

"Was there a 'We Shoot Trespassers' sign on any of them?"

The camper bumped over something that might have any of a dozen rural threats to a new tire's integrity. JT dashed off a silent prayer to the BFGoodrich corporate office.

"What was that?" Katy said.

"Ran over something," JT said.

"Well, stop," she said.

The cab shuddered as if passing over washboard ruts, and JT decided to stop. The camper was about two-thirds across the property line, and he'd be hacking through corn stalks in another few feet.

"Look," he said. "Stopped. It ain't trespassing in an emergency. If somebody got lost or hurt on his land, the owner either knows about it or needs to." He flipped on the high beams.

They had wasted precious minutes patrolling the area where the camper had been parked, flashing lights, blowing the horn, and calling Bobby and Lisa by name. JT hoped, and reassured Katy with as much optimism as he could muster, that one of them had sprained a leg and was laid up at the kindly farmer's house for shelter. The picture of shelter in his mind was less than cozy, given the infestation of malicious crows and the ominous confines of the green-maize fortress. Any other explanation for Bobby and Lisa's lateness was bound to be worse.

Katy gripped JT's shoulder, as if she'd seen something pass through the light. A second later, JT saw something else. Off to their right, the greenery formed a massive cobweb shape.

Black bird shapes littered the web, heads hanging limply from their necks. Whoever kept the grounds had a bizarre sense of artistry, or else the cornfield itself had developed its own self-defense tricks. JT had no wish to discover the truth.

Someone had cut a broad lane through the corn, too far in and over to risk rolling the camper that far, but enough to offer a view through the crops to the homestead beyond. The clouds that seemed to have left the state for days had returned to blot out the stars, leaving only the sallow unblinking eye of the moon. JT could swear he'd seen stars earlier, but the closest thing to a star was the wink of light from the low silhouette of the farmhouse a good distance across the property.

"Looks like they're not keeping farmer's hours tonight," said JT.

"That doesn't worry you?" Katy asked. She fixed her eyes on a large barn jutting against the indigo sky.

"Katy," JT said with measured calm. "I think I'm on record as not liking any of this one bit. We have enough sense to agree on that. But a light in the window is the best sign we have that somebody's sitting up late with company, maybe waiting for us to come collect our strays and move on down the road. I sure as hell won't camp on this land tonight, even if they invite us, which I don't expect…"

He stopped, as the light in the farmhouse winked out. Darkness and silence took over.

"Shit," said JT, and killed the engine.

"What about the lights?" Katy said, although she didn't sound eager to have them turned on again.

"Let me think," he said.

It took him a minute or two of intent listening to realize the most unnerving thing about their situation. The absence of bugs on such a wide swath of country land put him off. Neither katydid nor cricket, singing chigger or whatever Western Nebraska could furnish in the way of night song made itself heard. With nothing but a faint breeze rustling the corn like a paper sea, his mind sat coiled in expectation of whatever lurked in the dark. He thought of the light someone had extinguished at their approach, after drawing them in—the trailing end of a thought that had slipped in too quickly for him to shut out. An image wriggled across his brain, plucked from one of Lisa's endless nature tirades. During a construction delay in Iowa she'd lectured them on anglerfish, godawful monstrous things that prowled the depths and shook a glowing lure for small fish, coaxing them in range of long nightmare teeth.

"Fucking fuck's sake," JT muttered. It was directed at himself, indignation at the chilly sweat he had squeezed from his forehead.

Katy gave him a look of resentment, clearly thinking the comment was somehow for her benefit. She opened her mouth for a sharp answer, and JT would not have minded hearing it, but a leafy crash from outside stopped her. Something large had tripped in the corn, righted itself, and continued moving through it.

JT, Katy mouthed.

He patted her hand, and together they moved out of their seats toward the rear cabin. JT stacked his left fist atop the right one, and made a slow lateral twitch of his wrists. His tension eased when Katy understood immediately, bending noiselessly at the knees and taking Bobby's baseball bat from the floor. The Slugger trembled in her grip, but she returned his uneasy grin when he rested his hand on her shoulder. Then he picked up the shotgun, chambered a shell, and slipped two more into the pump magazine with a skill he had not forgotten from his compulsory boyhood instruction in duck hunting.

Disembarking, JT noticed a pallor like yellow wax cast by the moon over everything. It was too much light for a night without stars, and too sickly. He would rather have seen less.

Even Katy, keeping alongside him, looked less wholesome than usual by the weird moon glow. When she switched on her blue dime-store flashlight, the artificial beam held far more appeal.

"Bobby!" JT called, a welcome break in the silence. He had not heard movement since leaving the camper, but thought this might stir the inertia of anything creeping around.

"B-bobby!" Katy faltered at first but found strength in her voice.

The two alternated calls for Bobby and Lisa. The occupants of the house could not ignore that forever, and the two reluctant scouts were armed to negotiate.

"Bobby, last chance," JT said. "If you're jacking with us, I may shoot you, but I'll make sure you live."

"Lisa!" Katy yelled.

"And Lisa, if screwing with us was your idea, I'll still only shoot Bobby."

"Bobby!" Katy hollered with all her might.

Finally, something stirred. It seemed to have moved farther from the camper. JT did not care for that.

"Hey, out there," he called. "If you speak English, we're not here for trouble. My brother's lost around here someplace, and his girl. We're here to pick them up."

Silence answered, then some ambiguous crunching. It could still be an animal, but what kind and how big?

"JT," Katy said, "we need more light. Put yours on."

For once he did not have a snappy answer. "Okay then," he said, snapping on the red plastic light and gripping it against the shotgun barrel with his thumb.

They had progressed a hundred feet or so along the edge of the corn. Now JT stepped to his right, disappearing quickly among the rustling corn.

"JT!" Katy called.

"I'm not going in deep. Just a little ways to check. Keep your light out ahead of you and I'll keep an eye on it. We'll go parallel, and you keep your eyes on that house as we get closer. See if anything moves in the yard."

Katy appeared to think it over, then started walking again.

JT listened for more sounds but could not hear much over his own clumsy progress. Watching Katy's light and doing his best to keep pace with her while scanning all around, he walked flat into a standing post. There was no scarecrow on it, like the one JT had seen earlier in the day, but a dull rank smell of dirt and straw lingered here. Perhaps it had been scarecrow-rotating day on the farm. Maybe it was only the mulchy funk of vegetable rot and rebirth.

Off to his side, Katy said something.

"What?" he replied, seeing that she had stopped a few dozen steps ago.

"I said there's a big cut patch here," she said. "Corn's all tied up in hunks."

"In what?"

"Bundles. I don't know. Hunks of corn?"

"Shocks," JT said. "Or sheaves. Hunks. I don't know either." He thought he heard her laugh, despite their shared apprehension.

Shining his light through slowly, he could see that seven bundles of stalks sat ready for gathering, along with a scatter of plants harvested but not yet bound up in the heavy, moldy rope. A number of rakes, blades, and other tools lay where they appeared to have been dropped, not the sort of job you would have expected to see lying around unfinished on a farm at night. Maybe Bobby's arrival had interrupted the end of day chores. But if that were true, where had everyone gone?

"JT," Katy, said, "I'm not sure we…" and she stopped. Her light rested on a small, vivid object against the black earth. "JT!"

"What?"

"Come back this way. Not straight to me. Bear left."

She guided him back toward the thing she had seen, the object not belonging to nature, even such a disordered nature as they had found there.

"I'm not seeing anything."

"On the ground. Look down! There." She whirled her light around as grass twitched behind her. By the time her beam had returned, JT had found the thing and knelt on the ground to study it.

"JT?"

He turned his face toward her light, and he could tell that his expression did not reassure her. He picked up the object and held it over his head, where she could see it clearly.

JT's hand cradled a small, bright pink shoe. It was Lisa's, and both of them knew it. Katy backed away, her face twisted in horror. "Lisa," she whispered, and then she shrieked. JT saw something come alive at her feet. A crow with an elongated body and shriveled wings wriggled like a worm in the dirt, cackling at her in fury. Seconds later, five or six birds emerged from the foliage to add their reproachful voices.

Katy dropped her light and shouldered the bat. JT saw her swing in a sharp downward chop, as if at a sinking ball. They had played together in more than one softball beer league, and she'd always had a weakness for chasing curves. He heard a choke and a squawk from the bird, and its body rolled almost to his feet, dead as a cannonball.

The other crows fled, screeching in alarm. Most ran or crawled in the dirt, but one had sufficient wing power to get semi-airborne like an escaping chicken. JT dove aside to avoid catching a face full of black taloned feet. Falling to one knee, he turned as it piled up against an obstacle. He thought the bird, like him, had struck a post.

What he saw instead was a rangy man-shape in filthy dungarees and plaid work shirt, a torn felt hat crowning the head. It gripped the squirming, protesting crow in leather-gloved hands and seemed to study it. Swinging his light, JT saw that the face had a rough and featureless texture, the outer skin some kind of sack or canvas. It chilled him, but what happened next shook him.

With a burst of savage might, the veiled farmhand—or scarecrow?—tore the bird into ragged halves, its thumbs hooked in to separate the ribcage. Wet innards hit the dirt like a dropped mouthful of stew. The figure cast the gory fragments away, no longer interested. The other fugitive crows tore at its knees, almost toppling it once before it began stomping them flat with awkward, heavy-booted feet.

"Katy, run." JT must have said it louder than he meant to, because she whirled and bolted as though fire had touched her. He cut to his right, aiming to intercept her on open ground and reach the camper together as quickly as they could.

As Katy turned to orient herself, outlined by her dancing flashlight, a broad flailing shape burst from the corn between them. An arm in tattered flannel grabbed for her hair, then pawed at her neck. Some twisted rural types were playing a night game, and JT did not care for it any more than he imagined Katy did. He prepared to cut in her direction at a run, but she gripped the bat's barrel parallel to her forearm and jabbed backward with it. The head of the bat struck below her attacker's ribs where tender guts ought to have been. The impact was dull, a sort of thud and then a crunch, but the figure did not double over or slow its pace. It grappled the bat and yanked.

"Katy," JT yelled. "Get low! Get low fast!" Despite the tendency to swing low outside her strike zone, she'd always listened to her base coaches and adapted quickly on the run. Tonight was no exception; she hit the dirt without hesitation. The silent stranger in the hefty boots tromped directly over her body, narrowly missing her head.

Terrified of killing his wife in the confusion, JT had waited for her to take his signal before shooting. Even with her safely out of his firing line, he couldn't steady his nerves. He jerked the trigger and missed the shot.

A second scarecrow moved in low to the ground, bulkier than the reedy crow killer JT had spotted first. It started after him with vigor, desperate to lay hands on him.

"Katy," he cried, "keep moving!"

"JT?" she called, on her feet now, swinging her light.

"Don't stop for me! Start the engine and gun it when I say!"

She took off without another word. From the corner of his eye, he watched her make the remaining distance unmolested, slamming into the side of the camper with her outstretched palms before throwing the door open.

In his peripheral vision, something unseen shook the corn. JT made a hip shot to ward off whatever might be coming. The scarecrow was almost upon him when he shouldered his firearm for a third shot. The close-quarters blast made contact at the shoulder, spinning the hooded attacker where it stood, tearing its left arm free. Ragged meat lay beneath, but disturbingly little blood. Weak bubbles, dark and syrupy, burst from the wound instead of arterial spray. Rather than pause to survey the damage more, JT lowered his shoulder and plowed over the thing, much the way it had blundered over Katy but with more calculated malice in his heels.

"Go, go, go!" he said, hauling himself up into the camper.

Katy relayed this order to the camper as she found the keys in the ignition and cranked it. "Go, go!"

The small cardboard box of shotgun shells was open on the small built-in table. Grabbing the door well with one hand to brace for acceleration, JT crooked the gun in his elbow and reached for a reload, just in case. The engine roared, together with what sounded like a triumphant bellow from Katy. In the next instant, an earthquake knocked them both from their perches. Katy pitched forward into the windshield, not hard enough to break it but with force enough to daze her. JT lost his grip on the ammunition, and heard shotgun shells clatter in all directions like an upset sack of dominos.

"Fahh…" was all he managed to say. Propping himself on shaking knees, he hunted blind until his fist closed around one of the cartridges. Outside, something was still coming.

"It won't go, JT!" she said. The engine screamed, and the camper lurched forward. Everything had gone wrong, and the problem could not be fixed from inside.

The scarecrow thrust its arm at the door, trying to step into the cabin. Even struggling for balance, JT had plenty of time to feed the action, chamber the shell, and fire.

The report of the gun inside the vehicle put a sharp ring in his ears and a cold ache in the center of his forehead. He searched the floor with his hand again, watching the torn body in the dirt. The scarecrow's grip had wrenched the camper door half off its hinges. JT could see the ruin of its chest and throat, amazed the head had not rolled away with so little left to hold it on. Finding another shotgun shell, he wasted no time loading it, though his quaking hands made the task difficult.

"Katy," he said.

She moaned, probing a cut on her forehead. "I'm here."

"I got it. That one anyway. I'm gonna check and see what's blocking us."

"Don't go out," she said.

"Sit tight."

The shell was in the gun, but JT waited to pump the chamber shut until he was outside. This time he wanted to send a clear "don't fuck with me" signal to anyone else nearby.

"Hear that?" he called into the night. "Anybody wants a mouthful of that, I got plenty."

Nothing answered his bluster. The other scarecrow, and whatever else, had either withdrawn or chosen to keep still. Running his eyes down the side of the vehicle, he saw without any difficulty that a heavy tool on a long pole, some kind of felling axe or maybe a sling blade, was driven deep into the front tire. The air went out of him, because he had known in his rational core somewhere. There was no need to walk the perimeter to guess that whatever had gotten to one tire had taken them all out. He saw the rear, the one he had just changed, impaled in a similar way. He could not identify the object sunk into the sidewall. It looked like a sharp bone.

He kept careful watch as he approached the scarecrow he had shot. Rather than leave himself open on every side, he gripped the motionless form by one rough rawhide overshoe and dragged it toward him, keeping his back against the camper.

The thing had real dead weight despite the profusion of corn husks filling out its clothes. A substantial frame supported it, not some fanciful Land of Oz nonsense. The shoe slipped free in his hand and when he dropped the leg, a ghost-pale but intact human foot hit the ground. Poking from the filth-matted pants, it took away all illusions of some Halloween prop come murderously alive. The foot was swollen like a corpse's, dark veins running like spidery gangrene branching through it, but it was a man's.

The shot-torn shoulder and neck, too, had been living tissue. White bone peeked through purple flesh near the top of the spine, causing bile to bubble in JT's empty stomach. Spilling from the half-destroyed throat were unmistakable kernels of corn, enough to clog a sizable pipe, sticky with something dark like burned engine oil but with a foul odor he could not identify.

"JT?" Katy called.

"Oh…" he stammered, "okay, I'm okay, honey. I'm j-just having a look at things."

"I don't see anybody, at the house or…"

"Stay put, Katy. Be up in a minute."

Resting a hand on the scarecrow's abdomen, he felt it crackle. That made him sick again. The thing was partially stuffed, mainly where its heavy innards ought to be. He had a sudden vivid picture in his imagination, not a stomach or bowels but a single swollen craw like a bird's, swaddled in a nest of old corn husks and brimming with more of that evil slime-blackened corn.

All this grotesque new detail was dull and cottony, filed on a high shelf in his mind, because his attention fixed on the buzzing alarm at first seeing the scarecrow's foot. Sickness twisted up from his stomach to his throat before he fully took its meaning. If he had not recognized the broad sole, high arch and stubby toes, distinctive even on a cadaver, he might have resisted lifting the burlap sack off the head.

In one dying cell of his heart, JT had known. Looking at the desecrated face of what he had finally killed, the creature that had pursued him in desperation, a scream began and resonated through his constricted chest before leaving his throat.

The skin of Bobby's face hung slack on the skull, perhaps where teeth had been broken or his whole jaw caved in. There was no easy way to be sure of this, nor of the expression he had worn in living death under his ghastly hood, because of the coarse black sutures that sealed his eyes and mouth shut. Whether his brother, after some horrid ordeal, had been left the power to cry out or the presence of mind to beg for rescue, was a mystery JT would have to live with. Or die.

The scarecrows came, of course. Whether awaiting an obscure signal or checked by cruel curiosity about what JT would do, they had held off until his cry of anguish tore the dark open. A deeper darkness fell, as if a stray cloud had found the moon at last. As the light vanished from before him, JT fired at the first row of advancing figures, hoping he might catch Lisa with a lucky shot and send her to any heaven or hell better than this. The muzzle flare was the last light he saw for some minutes, charging to meet the scarecrows, wielding the gun as a club. He connected with a few heads, and then there were more hands on him than he could swim against, and he left the ground.

He had dim impressions of Katy calling to him, and him calling to her, certain she would get some good licks in with the bat. But given such a poor occasion to grieve his brother, he had trouble keeping his mind in the moment as he was borne aloft on the rough-shirted shoulders of ghouls. Many minutes of fumbling and shouting passed before he was aware of a light glowing before him. Someone in the house was awake again, and had lit a new lamp.

The scarecrows made their way along well enough without eyesight, voicing no grunts or curses as they carried him up to the porch. They only rustled with a faint, swarming insect sound, so it startled JT when the twisted shape lurking in the doorway spoke.

"More company for vittles, Mother."

PART TWO: UPON THIS ROCK

(TWO YEARS AGO)

CHAPTER ONE

Wings of a Dove

Marcie Baker set her shoulders and threw her weight against the yoke, suddenly afraid that her aircraft would refuse to pitch the way she told it to pitch.

"Come on," she hissed to the Citabria, which wrestled her as if part of its tail had come loose and jammed the elevators. Cold sweat burned Marcie's right eye until she had to squeeze it shut. "Come on, son of a bitch!"

Something responded to her third or fourth curse. The plane lurched, almost toppling into a dive. She trusted reflexes and muscle memory to keep stable, yet her expertise could do nothing to remedy an abrupt fuel shortage. She would have to land before she went down.

There were plenty of strips Marcie would sooner have chosen for an urgent night landing, many of them smaller than the municipal airport at Wallace, Nebraska. She had only breezed through Wallace once, maybe twice before. She did not know the territory, nor how things might be run on the late shift. The only advantage was that the place happened to be underneath her at a crucial time.

Late-night legs were not her habit, but she had been eager to get home after the refuel stop in Lenora, a rusty buttonhole of a town where life after sundown was dull at best, eerie at worst. She had been late out of Lawrence Muni and ought to have spent the night before starting fresh. In some vague way Kansas had put her off. She did not understand the Midwest. Never mind that unless she landed with care, she could become a permanent topographical feature.

The wind had given her hell for an hour, far more than the weather reports and her experience at the throttle warranted. The aircraft, although not her own, was a model she had flown dozens of times. Ever since her Lenora takeoff something had lagged in the maneuvering, beyond the usual stiffness of operating a borrowed bird. She'd had all weekend to get accustomed to it, dropping off a freshly minted pilot to take possession of his newly purchased plane. Marcie was fifteen years a flight instructor, and a pilot a hell of a lot longer than that. Instinct, or something subtler, ought to have made her check the works once more before departing, but her primal brain had been busy telling her to get the hell out of northwest Kansas and back to Wyoming.

She thought of Clay McAvoy, the gangly old pirate with whom she shared regular off-duty drinks and, about six times a year, her bunk. He would be waiting at Converse County Airport, hours early, nearly as eager to greet his returning companion as to see his beloved Citabria safe and sound. Never would he suspect the craft might unaccountably lose control, burning far too much fuel for the airspeed and range of the trip. Without warning, Marcie had found herself well outside self-imposed safety parameters for flying other people's planes.

"Wallace Ground," she said carefully into the radio, remembering to recite Clay's aircraft ID, not her own. She wished for her Bellanca Scout, laid up in the shop back in Douglas and unable to help her now.

For several seconds too long, the airwaves were dead. She was about to hail a second time when a sleepy voice responded.

"Citabria 1325, this here's Wallace Ground. Go ahead."

Marcie's held breath rattled out of her, replaced by giddy distress. Emergency protocols chimed in her head, commanding her to call for precautions, clear the runway, and phone the fire wagon. She shook out all that clanging debris, realizing what rattled her most was the prospect of having to get Clay's plane repaired. She was on her way down. After a certain point, it was up to fate and the east wind. She had no reason not to fly by the rules that had got her this far.

"Wallace Ground, 1325 east Wallace, three miles. Information Bravo. Inbound for landing."

Marcie allowed herself a whoop of relief as she climbed from the cockpit. Just before touchdown, as she grappled with the rudder to point a straight approach, the Citabria had bucked off its ailment with a bump and come in smooth as a butter knife. Her elation at having survived made her forget about being stranded in the uncertain arms of a town called Wallace, a whole state line away from home, until mechanics could have a proper look at the plane.

As soon as the prop spun down, she turned and saw two people emerge from a low-roofed aluminum building. They ran across a wide patch of desiccated grass to the runway. The first was a wiry red-haired chickenhawk of a man, coming at an urgent lopsided trot with a fire extinguisher held in front of him. The other, a doughy towheaded kid, jogged behind at a less anxious pace. He carried a push broom.

"Shit almighty, Citabria!" shouted Red as he huffed up to Marcie. "You all right?"

"I am now," said Marcie, smiling. "Glad you guys kept the porch lights on."

The man shook his head, as though she had not understood his question. "What the hell was that shook loose from your aircraft?"

Marcie cocked her head, "Shook loose? Oh, I just had some controls freeze up on me, and my airspeed bottomed out. That's why I had to bring her down. Have you got somebody who—"

Red was already circling the plane. "Damnation," he said, "I thought one of your dern wings had come off"

"The plane's all together, I think. I'll need to have someone look it over before I fly again. Too late tonight, obviously."

The kid stood clutching his broom, managing to look confused and bored at the same time. Evidently, he had come along under orders and had not seen what the older man had.

Red threw his hands up. "A storage bay must have fell open on you, then. You ain't..." He narrowed his eyes. "Y' ain't carrying nothing I don't want to know about, are you?"

Pink fire burned in her cheeks. "Mister," she said, "I'm carrying nothing but a duffel bag and I don't care who knows about it." If Barney Fife wanted to see her toothbrush and spare drawers, Marcie had no qualms about presenting them.

"Okay, okay then." Red screwed up his face like he was attempting long division. "I guess...hell... I'm stone sober, but I saw something bounce off you when you landed."

"Hey, yo." The kid spoke up in a tone that instantly let Marcie know he was baked. He pointed to a dark shape on the runway, just visible, about two hundred yards back. A black trail smeared the tarmac apron behind it.

"Ah, shucks," said Red with an elaborate know-it-all nod. "There it is. You must've clipped a doe with your landing gear. Don't happen much, but it happens. Lucky you."

"Lucky me," Marcie said. The curled mass was big enough to be a deer, but to her eye the dimensions weren't right.

"Seriously," Red said, "that coulda been a bad deal for everybody. We shoot 'em like crazy out here. In season, of course. I never saw one on a runway this late in the year, though."

Marcie hoped this bossy little man had left someone in charge of the radio. Still, clearing the runway was a priority. Before she could offer to taxi the Citabria to a hangar, the three of them went to make sure that the animal was dead.

"I'll have to grab the tractor and shove it into the grass for now," said Red. Marcie wondered what the man would do if the deer was not entirely dead. Brain it with the push broom, perhaps. Or make the boy do it.

Up close, the deer was no deer. It lay still as a rock but slumped over in a posture that made Marcie's blood change temperature. The body was not precisely human, nor was the coarse hair along its back that of any familiar animal.

"Oh, Lord," Red whispered. "Lord Jesus."

Marcie realized she was nodding. Lord Jesus indeed.

"Is it, like, dead?" said the kid, not catching the full import. Before the other two could speak, he prodded the mass with the head of his broom.

On the third jab, the thing breathed. It made the sound a shovel head makes when dragged over gravel. Long limbs unbent, and the three witnesses looked into the pus-yellow eyes of a bipedal creature taller than any of them had ever seen.

"Oh, no," Red said, an octave lower than before. "No."

That was the last word spoken. Two seconds later, the kid's broom smacked against Red's head and he reeled semi-conscious to the ground. The kid's hand still clasped the broom handle, attached to a forearm terminating in red pulp. The severed limb trailed a skinny muscle that plopped against Red's chest like a warm tongue.

Marcie gaped at the stowaway, leaden from the waist down as she watched it skin the young man's body with a series of haphazard rips. Only when she retched with incoming nausea did it notice her. Cradling the boy's raw carcass-meat in a protective wing, it lashed the castoff skin at her face like a gladiator's net.

When Marcie fell, she struck her left temple on the tarmac. Her unconsciousness was the only mercy, because she did not have to witness the feast that followed in the dark. It had no ceremony and brought no satisfaction, leaving (as always) a greater hunger than before.

CHAPTER TWO

I Am a Pilgrim

The traveler did not waste time hiding the carnage. It was beyond caution, approaching the end of its endurance. The putrefying remnant of its mind could barely form a memory of why it had been sent. Its cracked feet kept moving not by reason or might but by instinct. In its present state, it had been rash to attempt air travel, but the prospect of making a few hundred easy miles had been too beguiling.

At the start of its recollections, in a limestone cave near the southwestern verge of Texas, it had journeyed forth holding a rugged form, rough and handsome, the kind of man-shape that foolish people found easy to trust. With endless lies and a gambler's luck, it had begged and borrowed its way, stealing outright when possible. It fed when quarry could be lured, rutted when the prey could be caught alone. The feeding was for survival, and its cravings increased as it filled itself. The desecration of men, of women, of stray animals, were a compulsion.

From within came the command to scar the earth in its tracks. For all its elaborate trappings it was a spore, charged to press on as far as it dared before taking seed. As it degraded into an ugly shadow, the servant of warring appetites, places of shelter became scarce and the suspicious glances of others bred danger. Inconsequential people were capable of swarms that could overpower or fatally slow it. Even in decline it wielded monstrous brawn and wits, but had no servile hordes to call upon. Allies were promised, in legions no less, but only these it could spawn for itself, later.

It had been reckless to venture into Dallas, merely the outskirts but still under the glow of metropolitan light. The traveler was a thing suited to wilderness, conjured from a hell-world of snakes and sand. The more it encountered the pulse and stink of humanity, the more it lurched between desire and repulsion. It had begun to bleed in public, no longer healing with ease. When walking the streets, it barely had strength to hold its unraveling aspect together. Whores, thieves and dogs began to scorn it for a broken-down clubfooted drifter. It wasted good hunting time fighting off less and less worthy assailants.

The traveler could remember scores of rats, rancid meat marinated in piss and diseased offal. Hiding in sewers from armed men, mewling for fresh blood like a blind kitten, it had contemplated drowning itself in the effluent rivers under Dallas. It had tasted a dozen flavors of the city's despair, but the pull of its master-voice like a bellyful of stinging insects goaded it onward.

In the godless wastes of Oklahoma, the traveler had experienced a brief and curious rejuvenation, despite its eroding sense of direction. By then it crawled only at night. It could hold its human disguises for no more than a few seconds. It had clung to the undersides of big trucks, the scales of its back soon scraped raw by asphalt.

In lucid moments, it clung to foretellings of hardier generations that would walk the same path, better adapted to the journey. If the traveler could find a foothold in some desolate place, a waypoint for those that followed, it would have done well.

By Kansas, the skin had worn thin enough to crack and tear as it walked. Limbs like reeds jittered in the wind, hollow as bird bones. Pouchy skin trailed it like flaccid wings. It spent a night and a day in a squalid rest area, listening to wet degenerate sounds. Every sordid coupling the traveler interrupted offered twice the nourishment in one sitting. In many cases it sensed that the dominant human had meant to murder its weaker mate, once their pleasure-making was finished. This was merely a detail to notice. A thing without conscience needed no balm.

Fortified by gorging, the traveler felt bold enough to brave the open sky. It had slept in high weeds along an airstrip, annoyed by the buzz of propellers. By then it could not show itself even at dusk, but slowing afternoon traffic had made it fearful of losing its chance until dawn.

The small blue airplane held only one passenger, but the traveler saw no easy way to hide under the fuselage before takeoff. To avoid detection, it had loped beside the aircraft just outside the runway lights, matching taxi speed until the tiny wheels left earth. It nearly missed the grab, snagging one talon in a wing flap, pulling itself flat and batlike against the airplane's cold belly.

In its overfed euphoria, the traveler judged its chances by an outdated estimate of itself. Scarcely had the plane leveled off when its limbs began aching with strain. Frigid wind caught and dragged on its sagging dorsal mass. Only by constant shifting and resettling had it managed to maintain a grip, while the little craft thrashed as if to shake the parasite loose.

It had believed itself done for when the impact of landing jostled its grip loose. The remaining skin flaked off its ribs. It slid into a sticky heap and lay as if dead, not daring to stir. Only when the humans came, their scent stale but enticing, had its naked heart flapped and breath swelled its punctured lungs.

After tearing their flesh and consuming all it could, the traveler still shivered with agony and fatigue. Let those who came at dawn make what they would of the pulp it ground underfoot, the flecks of spine and skull painted across the little airplane's hull, the blood vomited in its gluttony. Spying what looked like a curious forest in the dark beyond the airfield, it went to hide.

The traveler found no sanctuary but a scratchy stand of withered corn. The stalks jabbed its gummy wounds, driving earth deep inside where infection could grow. It had learned to embrace pain, finding ecstasy in corruption. It no longer knew itself in a coherent form, mindless progress undoing the last of its reason.

By sunrise, clinging husks plastered the length of its sticky body, pulled from their brittle stems as the intruder passed. The Nebraska sun rose high and harsh, beyond the reach of any cloud. Beneath and around the bandaging husks, the last of the traveler's fragile flesh blistered with heat. Sores burned red and then black as it trudged on, heedless. Dry vegetable matter hardened and tightened over its running lesions like brittle armor. The mingling of its blood with the soil sent pulses of vitality deep within, triggering a metamorphosis. The traveler did not see the narrow ribbon of green in its wake. Drought-stunted grass and corn showed momentary renewal where its cooked blood fell, then turned brown and dead once more.

None saw the transformation except a pair of crows in a hackberry tree, fighting over a dead field mouse. They stopped their squabble to watch the black thing pass. One gargled a soft wary caw, then silence fell again.

CHAPTER THREE

We Plow the Fields and Scatter

The farmer awoke and dressed in the dark, careful not to disturb his wife. It was near enough rising time, but he wanted her to sleep as long as possible. Her brave smile was worked to the bone, and it hurt him to see. Weariness was making old folks of them.

He visited the barn first thing before every sunrise. Numerous occupations awaited him there. Small repairs, accounts to tally, matches to light and study as they burned down, meditations on God's goodness, dreams of new wells he would never dig, pleas to God, profanities to hurl at God's baffling designs, and scores of rats to kill whenever he found them, led the farmer each morning to reflect on self-annihilation. He had figured nine sure ways of ending his life in the barn, where his wife would find him eventually but not soon enough to save him. His aim in sketching these unsavory plans was to talk himself out of suicide, but surely one day he would talk himself into it by mistake.

The farmer and his wife were born to subsistence, never starving and never thriving. It would have been simpler never to taste prosperity, for nothing made hard times harder than memories of hope. Years ago, youth and promise had baited them with ambition. He had been a good farmer, a good husband, a good citizen, and she his good wife. They had been everything good except father and mother, a drought having nothing to do with the weather but just as keenly felt on long summer days, as the two of them worked their land like lonesome ants. The farm's yield sustained them, along with a few animals. It could do no more.

The barn was silent, without even the familiar sounds of the old milk cow breathing and breaking wind in her sleep. The farmer's nose flared at a peculiar tang overlaying the dull farmyard musk, as if something had been bleeding in the dark.

Before he reached the cow in her stall, his eye fell on a shriveled figure in the far corner. It was like a mummy, or something of that sort, made of black broken twigs. Twine and sacking bound it together.

No, he thought, *not sacking*. It was corn wrapped about the thing, all silk and dry shucks.

A damp, musty voice entered the farmer's mind. It was the voice that sometimes urged him to drink lye or hang himself from the loft, or else a clever mimicry of that voice. Now it told him to run, but he was used to ignoring its advice. The hideous corn-and-straw doll bewitched him. He wondered who had put it in his barn, whether some neighbor meant it as a joke or a hex. All but a few of the other sodbusters had pulled up stakes, hollered uncle to the drought and moved on as if there were some other place they stood a chance of doing better. So much for tradition. So much for working the native soil, godly patience and respect be dashed.

A rank breeze tousled his thin hair, and he shuddered. The air must have come through a crack in the barn, but the farmer itched with certainty that the desiccated intruder had exhaled on him. A hay fork leaned against the near wall, its tines knobbed with rust and manure. He picked it up before stepping closer.

A loud caw jangled him. Looking up, he spied a god-blighted crow peering at him from the hay loft.

"Just you wait 'til I'm done here," he said in a tone of spite equal to its hostile squawk. Defending what good corn he had left from the black pest-birds was a source of primal joy, strengthening him against melancholy. He took another step toward the contorted oddity in the corner.

The crow cawed again.

"Git on to hell," said the farmer, "or by fire, I'll put you there."

The crow kept up its noise, letting off a chirp about every two seconds, a low steady call of alarm like the farmer had never heard birds make before. Another crow, outside the barn, started up in its own cockeyed rhythm. A third followed. The farmer anticipated a full day of crow shooting, once he'd speared the weird effigy and cast it off his property.

He'd been afraid that the thing, dead as it looked, might open its eyes. When the misshapen head tilted upright on its own, he realized its eyes were already open. Black sockets yawned with the same hunger as the foul gash of its mouth. The farmer's voice rose as it had not since his boyhood days in church, a quavering scream drowned by the sudden cacophony of crows.

Half a dozen birds came swooping in at the eaves of the loft and circled in an attack pattern. Gouts of bird shit rained down. The husk-thing thrust embracing arms around the farmer to crush him, but the exhausted limbs quivered and splintered under their own force.

The farmer shut his eyes and jabbed from the shoulders, aiming for the creature's throat. In the middle of his lunge the figure stood upright, presenting a concave belly to the fork tines instead. The blow unplanted the heavy clawed feet, but the horrid body pitched forward. The farmer fell on his back, throwing his arms upward so that the fork handle missed punching through his forehead by inches. He blinked at the creature skewered above him, its jaw slack, releasing a flood of noxious black muck. The corruption the traveler had given its whole being to transport spilled over the farmer's head, running in his eyes, clogging his nose and throat. He choked and gagged, trying without success to heave it back up.

The crows dove, jabbing their beaks at the vile shape sliding down the fork's handle. They seemed to know it as their enemy, tearing its corn-husk flesh as it descended to rest atop the farmer like a lover from beyond the grave. The jabbing beaks failed to do much damage, but they continued their frenzied pecking for several minutes.

The farmer, caked in black slime, rolled and found his feet. He twisted with savage effort, pulling his weapon free of the monster's torso. Before the crows could organize themselves again, he batted one from the air with lethal force, then pinned another to the barn's hard earth floor. The others escaped, calling out in terror.

The farmer jabbed his fork again and again into the dissipating flesh of the devil he had killed, frantic at the thought of its regurgitated bilge inside him. After a minute or two of stabbing, he slowed his rhythm and paid heed to a sound like a gentle whisper. It came from the same place as his mocking suicidal conscience, but the voice had changed.

Do not fear.

A foolish thing to be told in the midst of a nightmare, but it had a seductive tone such as the desperate might wish to believe.

Grow. For the harvest, grow. Do not fear.

He not only heard the voice but felt it, a cool caress on the back of his head. No longer mindful of drought or the treacherous east wind, he shivered with the promise of something new arriving.

Do not fear. Grow.

A short time later, the farmer stood at the edge of his best cornfield. It was hardly enough to be called a crop. The ears bowing the brittle stalks would not be worth the trouble of selling them. He and his wife would soon choose between feeding the cow, the laying hens, or themselves.

He stood in silence, awaiting a sign from the presence bonding itself to him. The breeze gusted at his back, shaking the plants before him and rustling fallen husks underfoot. The breeze made a sound like *Grow.*

With one clammy hand he grasped a stalk. The surface that

met his palm felt smooth and lively. Without seeing, he knew it was green beneath his fingers. He withdrew the hand, put it to his tongue where the husk-devil's foul taste mingled with his own spit, and scooped out a dark glob like tar. He spread the resin over one slim, crooked ear of corn. He worked it lovingly like a salve, and was barely surprised when the husk grew supple in his hands. A light, healthy green crept into the silk as he rubbed in the strange blood across it with sensuous delight. The corn swelled obscenely under his touch until fat golden kernels peeked through, the ear nearly doubling in size as he watched and stroked.

The voice from within sank downward, embedding itself deeper in the farmer. It spoke three words.

For the harvest.

He went to the barn for his axe, looking at the cow as he passed her stall in the advancing light. The bloody devastation of her throat and belly showed where the dark intruder had fed before dawn, prior to its torpid rest against the wall where he had discovered it.

His wife appeared while he was in the yard sharpening the axe. Her clothes were disheveled and cross-buttoned, as if she had put them on in haste after a commotion or a bad dream roused her. He stared at her, his mind on chopping.

"Coffee's hot," she said, and set a chipped cup on the splitting stump for him.

"Something got in the barn," he said, and moved away without another word or a glance at his coffee. He turned his eyes away from the apprehensive questions on her face.

Once in the barn again, he straddled the grisly remains of his visitor with the axe upraised. He was calculating how many fragments he ought to scatter in the fields, and how far apart they should be sown, when the voice returned.

No.

The farmer released the axe and dropped his arms to his

sides. The words worked their way up, a chant rising from a deep muffled place.

Roots. Deeper. Roots. Deeper. Grow.

Roots? Was he to till up the ground and start fresh? There could be no planting in a summer drought. The farmer knew the stories of Job and Abraham, those hard-luck bastards tested in faith. He had made up his mind that he had no constitution for such trials.

"Won't be no roots if I tear 'em out," he muttered. The touch at the back of his head tightened as if to punish him, but eased off shy of dealing true pain.

Roots. Deeper, deeper. Another word, too soft to hear even in the quiet barn, rose from beneath him. Wafting up a long tunnel. A pit, or…

Well.

Within an hour, the farm offered a taste of its bounty.

His wife prepared a supper of beans boiled with old husks, their chief meal for as long as they could remember. Modest folks abided in modest times. He shoved the screen door open with his muddy boot, tracking rich black earth into the house, shoulders rolling under the weight of a swinging pail. He hoisted it onto the table, which looked in danger of buckling.

She turned and her eyes went big. "What's that you have there?" She knew perfectly well what it was, but manifestly could not believe her eyes.

"It's corn," the farmer said, beaming with a look that hurt his face after months drawn down in worry. "It's a true miracle, woman. Half a row just like this, ripe to bursting, in full summer."

They clasped hands and danced on the dirty kitchen floor, their mouths watering for the summer corn as their hearts rejoiced. They held one another tight until they fairly wept. They were delivered.

CHAPTER FOUR

In the Garden

The farmer was his old self again, for a time. Having given its order, the traveler's remnant crouched inside him to watch. It would not do for the farmer or his wife to think he was losing his mind. Just as well she had not seen him drag the withered husk-thing from the barn across the yard when she went to gather eggs. Better still that she had not seen him tip the black thorny mass into the well.

The farmer made an inconspicuous cut in his arm with a skinning knife, and squeezed out a modest blood offering to quicken the scant essence which lay inert in the brittle corpse. The sinews hissed as a bond sealed between the ruined aspect sinking into the groundwater and its living agent above. The well was good, one of the few treasures left on the farm, and the farmer did not expect his wife to grasp how his actions would improve it.

More than a usual number of crows loitered in the sky. He did not bother hiding his agitation from his wife. With a prize batch of miracle corn, what man would not be jealous of pests moving in? If the yield continued, they would both be put to hard work protecting it.

She'd always gathered old clothes worn thin with use. In the spirit of Christian frugality, she'd meant to patch and line them for wearing again. Good cloth was good cloth, and she raised no objection to clothing scarecrows with it, so long as nothing went to waste. The farmer raked fallen husks and straw the cow did not want, forming long piles roughly man-sized. Together they fashioned and filled their new sentries to ward off encroaching birds.

The farmer split a fallen tree, which he had meant for months to burn, into three stout posts and sank them in the dirt. He hung the strawmen, one at either end of the cornfield and a third at the place of honor in the middle. The sight of them gladdened his wife's face.

But the evil one was subtle, sending flights of wicked black birds upon the wind. For a few days, the crows balked at the three strange newcomers. After that, the enticement of new-risen corn already fattening in the sun overcame their fear.

The woman walked the rows with her husband, straightening and cleaning the scarecrows as he paced the dirt and thought his inscrutable thoughts. Her face wrinkled at the sight of his agitation, even in the midst of miracles, but she held her tongue and surely could not divine their inmost source.

Despite all efforts, the crows became accustomed to the hanging effigies. The corn was hardy but the birds came in greater numbers every week, snatching kernels off the ears. The farmer called them a sickness. His wife agreed, at first. She mentioned that crows had begun pestering her henhouse, pecking holes in the slats and scaring the poor hens out of healthy temperament. She seemed aggrieved that he had not noticed it for himself, but he had larger matters to ponder.

He began holding his one-sided conversations in the house, not before his wife but anytime she turned her back or left the room. He did not bother lowering his voice.

For her part, his wife began praying out loud for the redemption of what she dubbed his "troubled spirit." He paid little mind, for he could see that she was slower to accept the new order. She moved about her chores like a hunted thing, flinching at every crow's caw from sunrise to dusk. She carried a broom to beat them away from wherever they perched. He'd shown her how to pick them off from the window with his battered M14, but the rifle's reports frightened her almost as much as the birds.

The farmer knew his business. Let his wife hail the heavens for both their souls if it brought her comfort. She'd come from snake-handling river folk, who spoke right up to God as if He sat in the corner. Let her pray for pestilence to blight the birds, and consecrate the corn to feed only its rightful keepers and the progeny they brought forth. If she added the odd misguided litany for her husband's sake, believing him a man beguiled, what was that but a sign of her devotion to him?

She told him to his face, only once, that he must resist the pull of unnatural evils. There were crafty others, she declared, who spoke in voices very much like God's. Understanding her veiled condemnation of the traveler, the farmer struck the boldness out of her straightaway. After regaining her senses, she went back to bothering her God exclusively.

The traveler returned, and not uninvited. They needed more than hand-sewn scarecrows to outmatch the birds threatening the reborn yield. The farmer sent his own prayers out, although he was less sure of their direction. The prompt reply let him know he was not forsaken. The master heard.

The sickness had to be eradicated, or held at bay. The coming harvest would not wait, and the farmer must be ready to devote his whole self to it. He had no money to hire help. The last truckloads of mercenary hands had left anyway, seeking lighter work in greener country. His few remaining neighbors in the county struggled to work their own acreage. His prosperity would make them covetous, inclined to cheat or even kill him. The hour of their usefulness had yet to arrive.

The farmer walked his rows in the cool of the day, under his master's eye. The crows had laid waste to a broad swath of corn, and pulled the nearest scarecrow into pieces to show their spite. Their gluttony weighed them down until some crept along the ground like worms.

The traveler assumed an angry form, squeezing the farmer's brain with its unseen hand until blood ran down the inside of the man's skull. The farmer pitched forward in a fit, his tongue lolling on the black earth as his body writhed and seized. The toppled head of the scarecrow glowered into his contorted face.

Little one, replied the traveler with cold contempt. *See your false image abased. It only tempts the sickness, no more. Your labors invite scorn upon the harvest.*

"Wha—" murmured the farmer, an infant yet learning to speak to its elders. "What d'ye want?"

Kill this sickness. Not with sticks and straw. With bone and muscle.

He gasped for the air to reply. "We're...killing as many as we-"

Not you. The crops need you, need tending.

"But..." He squealed against his pain. "I'm tending. I'll tend it good. And m'wife."

The other may stay, the woman, if she will serve.

"I... I thank you..."

Grow, came the command with fresh agony. *Against the sickness, grow.*

"How? Sh-show me how."

The pain abated at these words. The farmer propped himself on shaking elbows. His nose dripped with blood. The droplets pattered softly on the torn sleeve of the mangled scarecrow's arm.

The two smallest of its gloved fingers curled.

The traveler whispered more, revealing its commandment in full, but the farmer knew everything in that spark of unholy animation.

"No," he dared to beg. He had embraced an awful thing, enslaved himself to its essence, but he had not expected to have true horrors asked of him.

The phantom grip jolted his head again, rough as the slap of a drunken mother.

Gather and grow, or die.

The brutality was real, for when the farmer awoke he could not move his neck without pain. Rising dirt-stained from the ground, he struggled for balance. An honest doctor would have told him the minor stroke he'd suffered was also real. With the rest of it, the vision, the commandment, he wrestled. The prayers of his wife restored him to reason as fully as he had been in months, long enough for him to recall his faith before the days of despair, before the monstrosity had first appeared in his barn. His clarity lasted long enough to remind him that deceivers had sweet voices, but holy signs would always reveal the right path.

No sooner had he finished the thought than a sign came to answer his doubt. He heard his wife screaming.

She had come for fresh eggs, refusing to abandon her hens despite their faltering yield. Dark slender crow-beaks probed at the henhouse opening to pluck feathers or draw blood. They seemed intent on driving the poor yard birds mad. The farmer, provoked more by hatred of the crows than by his concern for egg-laying, had helped her set sandpaper strips across the roof with nails driven through, pointed skyward to repel perching invaders.

With her constant smile wrinkled by fatigue, the pulse of hope feeble in her heart, she had looked faithfully after her pretty ones. Opening the coop door, she expected a chorus of hungry clucks. Instead, there came a frenzy of caws, and a cloud of feathery black dashed her to the ground. More crows than she could imagine poured from the rank henhouse confines and set upon her. She shrieked, flailing her egg basket until a black talon tore it from her with strength beyond what was natural or right.

One brash bird went for her eyes. She squeezed them shut, so it clawed through the lids. Blood oozed across her cheeks, nearly choking her as she cried for help and spat oily feathers away from her lips.

An instant later her husband appeared, brandishing his pitchfork. He shooed, skewered, and beat the ravaging crows until the stragglers retreated, calling threats of vengeance as they went.

The traveler left the farmer alone for a while, allowing him to help his wife inside to bed while its dire lesson sank home. She moaned like a sick child as he dressed her face and hands, nursed her through that night and the next without sleep. A hundred times the pestilent birds pecked at the roof and windows, bringing her out of howling nightmares into a blind world under seeping bandages. Every time he was there to take her hand, to feed her broth and soothe her terror.

He tended her with a thankful heart. If she had been spared, then she had been judged useful, and soon their bodies could both return to toil for the farm's sake. His mind was quiet, because he had received a sign. Protecting the farm for the harvest would take strength. Bone and muscle were needed to serve—not dumb effigies but creatures of substance.

To gather it was needful to grow; to grow it was needful to gather. And the growing had already begun.

CHAPTER FIVE

We Gather Together

She took her time getting out of bed and on her feet again. The lacerations over her arms and body were not as grave as they looked. She kept them as clean as she could, hoping they would not fester. The true damage was to her spirit, and of course her eyesight. The talons had scratched like brambles, leaving permanent slashes across her once-keen vision.

The effect was like peering at the world through a white slatted fence. The depth and distance of fixed objects teased her; she relied on things to move for her to see much of them. She prayed until her strained vocal cords gave out, and went on praying in her mind. Her husband became a rawboned shadow coming and going at sporadic intervals, to feed and wash her as needs demanded. He too whispered prayers, but she shut her ears to their ungodliness. The bounteous blessing light upon the farm had fallen among clouds. The divine eye she had trusted to watch over them seemed as blighted as her own.

Whatever burdens he shouldered on his own, she was not ready to venture back outside and help her husband keep the farm. When she faced the yard again, more crows would be waiting. Meanwhile, he awoke her at odd hours, to remind her of the outside world with inexpert meals concocted from corn and little else.

Where before she'd heard only the silence of a husband working deep in his field, she now heard the sounds of heavy labor around the yard and barn, as if structures were being shored up. Occasionally, she heard the blast of his rifle and the frenzy of wounded birds. Her heart thrilled to hear them suffer, but their cries wove shivering nightmares to ambush her when she dozed.

Her damaged eyes produced another strange effect. As her

husband grew more erratic in his care, she perceived his shadow becoming unstuck. The dark after-image flickered at his shoulders and heels. It was like him, but not entirely. It was more gaunt and forbidding, hunched over the flesh and blood of him with jealous hunger. The corrupted shade, which seemed to crouch and whisper at his ear, lent a horrible kind of sense to his constant, sullen muttering.

One day she heard his filth-caked boots tromp around the kitchen, to the porch, and back again as though something had agitated him fiercely. His voice found her in the back of the house, not his low imprecations but full-throated speech. He sounded apologetic, as if caught unawares by a visitor.

"Can't answer for the state of the place," he said, "only the wife's not been well."

Perhaps in his overworked state, he had outrun her to madness. Yet another voice, younger, one she had never heard, made a halting reply she could not discern.

A table overturned; she recognized the sound. The noise of a struggle followed, all stomps and scrapes. The stranger cried out, the sound muffled, a mouth roughly stopped by a gloved hand or the wiry crook of an elbow.

A hand fumbled at the door, someone's frantic attempt to enter her room. Her mind's eye pictured a robbery, her husband fighting off some caller who had turned on him. Her heart whispered a different story.

When the door crashed inward, spilling candlelight and a flailing human form, she avoided screaming by biting her lip down to a generous pocket of blood. The prone intruder was a young man, the sort they'd hire as a harvest hand any season they could spare the money. He too bled at the mouth, wailing incoherent pleas through broken teeth as he clawed the floor like a rat thrown onto a griddle. Someone had hold of his feet. His eyes shone in desperate appeal, as if she could have helped. She lowered her eyelids to slits, lest they shine back.

Her husband appeared in the doorway, spattered bloody and brandishing a short-handled hoe. He hooked the stranger at the junction of neck and shoulder, but other hands helped him drag the gasping body back into the kitchen. She heard at least two besides the farmer and his guest.

Later, after stillness returned, her husband entered the sickroom. He watched for many minutes without approaching the bed, as if measuring her consciousness and what she might have seen. When he shuffled to her bedside at last, his face quivered in a pained imitation of his older, more tender self. He spoke, or tried to, with reassurance and love, smoothing damp hair off her brow.

She made a diligent show of waking, with delicate flutters of her eyes.

"Lord, woman," he said with a rattle of amused relief in his throat, "you been thrashin' all night, burned up with fever. I reckon it's broke now."

"Was I dreaming?" she prompted – the question he surely hoped she would ask.

"Dreaming," he said with an over-wound mechanical nod. "I guess you have been. You hollered for me and swore a boy was being ki…dying right there in that door, with me standing by all the time."

It was clumsy cover, putting what she'd witnessed down to sickness and claiming she'd told it to him as a fever dream, the best effort of a man who'd never been handy with stories. He hovered over her, not with menace but desperate to have her believe. He wanted her to give a sign, speaking some fraction of the incident aloud.

"Yes," she said, "And oh! How funny that dream turned on me. You had a mess of corn you were cooking up, and some fool yelled out he didn't want none, like it was poison. And… even in my dream I thought 'How foolish,' not to take a hot meal of good crops like we got."

That brightened him right up. His brow unfolded and he relaxed his posture. "Aw, darlin' girl," he said with a familiar kindness that made her want to weep, she missed it so. "I've done such work on this place. It's a reg'lar new Eden, and we'll never again want nothin', you or I."

Abruptly, almost before finishing the sentence, he turned and started out of the room. Whatever dwelt beyond the door had summoned him. Assured that he had nothing to fear from her, he rushed to answer it.

Although she was the type of wife willing to keep a husband's secrets out of duty, she had not kept many of her own. Her show of unquestioning, defenseless gratitude for the farmer's careless ministrations endured long after the genuine feeling ceased in her. She hid all signs of the strength and wits that returned to her by daily degrees. The nourishment was poor and increasingly rancid, but gave her sufficient energy for slow healing.

She suspected that the well water he brought was especially tainted. She could not refuse it, but let it sit in the glass as long as she dared until a fine ashy silt settled out of the liquid. She drank as little of the dregs as possible, emptying the sloppy residue behind her headboard. Whether the precaution truly helped her constitution, or merely gave her courage to plan beyond a slow death, rare warmth kindled in her heart. Her faith held. Salvation could not be long in coming.

CHAPTER SIX

Bringing In the Sheaves

The farmer no longer had time to indulge in thoughts of himself, suicidal or otherwise. The farm bade him work, and though his heart was willing his hands bore the strain. The new helpers, baptized and remade in the farm's image, took over turning the soil and tending the rows. Finding new able bodies to convert for service fell to the farmer. Always more work and more hands needed, no matter how many bodies he rounded up.

Prowling country highways in his road-battered truck became a nightly chore. People were scant in the vicinity, and he dared not risk pushing into larger towns where too many missing would attract notice. Now and then his roving thoughts coalesced in regretful fancies of the life a brood of sturdy sons might have meant for them.

His greatest joy would have been to keep the family land in the family, and he hoped his newly strengthened essence would give him potency to sire children. If successful, splicing his lineage to the traveler's would be an acceptable compromise. Yet it was dangerous to wish for what was yet ungranted. It smacked of ingratitude.

He believed he had sown a child in his wife, once long ago, but that crop had not taken. Life had conditioned him to be stoic about misfortune, but their failed propagation went hard with him. He still cared for his wife, and for her sorrows, never meaning to use her badly when he did. Feelings were not all burned out of him, but in them he perceived how much of his will the traveler had consumed. It hardly needed to nudge his thoughts, for he reasoned and spoke for himself in the language of his new consciousness.

His rebel thoughts came as dreams, after which he remembered little but frequently woke up in staring panic, holding a good sharp knife and wondering if it would taste better than corn. Once, he contemplated severing his tongue to see whether the pain might purge him back to his dull old self. Not suicide but surgery.

Always he caught himself before the traveler caught him peering down forbidden roads and brought him back to obedience with a flick of its claws against his tender brain. That, above anything the farmer could inflict on himself, was pain. That was purification. Until he proved worthy of rearing sons, his charge would be to find acolytes where he could.

Drifting souls never failed to appear, given patience and time; humanity's chaff had survival instinct. Eating meant moving sometimes, and moving meant running out of road sometimes. The farmer drove longer distances each week, to be waiting at the end of that road when the unwary reached it.

He had collected one of his earliest and best specimens from the main route to the state line. The boy's burly frame indicated he was fit for hard work, and would have been a credit to the football team or military outfit of his choice. Had he not been so drunk, hoofing home along the roadside after some barn dance, the farmer might have had trouble with him. By that time, new recruits only had to be brought within the boundaries of the farm. From there, the helpers he had already made could tame all resistance and begin the rituals of conversion. The young man had not realized where he was before the work was as good as finished.

The farmer had known that boy. He belonged to odd folks who ran a roadside souvenir stand at the local filling station. They must have sold enough diesel and chewing tobacco to scrape by, for their cheap corn-themed attraction was too far out of the way for any but the rare passers through. The only time business picked up was during the little annual harvest fair, which had been a true festival in the farmer's nearly forgotten childhood, but had dwindled by degrees to nothing, like everything else in the county.

The truck shuddered gently as he eased the clutch for the long bend around the fairground lot. The vehicle had plenty of honest miles on it, like its owner, but continued giving reliable service even as fuel and cash to buy it grew hard to find. That had seemed the first obstacle to the farmer's expanding outfit.

When he first caught one of the scarecrows troweling the black-green secretion of his miracle corn into the truck's tank, he'd taken a kaiser blade to the obviously defective helper until it lay in tatters at his feet. To his astonishment, the truck burned that malodorous muck about as well as low-grade commercial fuel. Despite the rasping hum and thick dirty exhaust, it kept the engine running fairly clean. No sooner had the farmer made this discovery than three scarecrows replaced the dismembered one, the first to resume fueling and the others to bear away any reusable pieces of their comrade.

Beyond the quiet fairground, at the edge of town such as it was, the northernmost row of buildings lay empty. Most recently abandoned was old Clevon March's garage for small engines. Clevon's faded sign remained above the main bay doorway, though someone had made off with the massive door itself. The interior was a cavern bare of any resource but shelter.

The farmer had followed a hunch about a hitchhiker he'd spotted that morning, a fair piece down the highway—some incongruous hippie throwback, long-haired in olive green. Clear daylight and open environs had denied him any opportunity to approach undetected, but given the distance and the harshness of afternoon sun, Clevon's or someplace near would present the most inviting haven. If the hiker was fool enough to walk all day, he should be predictable enough to stop for the night. He wished a burly, reasonably expendable scarecrow could have come along to help him, but their lifeblood was bound to the home soil. Besides, he had no wish to answer for their behavior out in the open world.

He positioned his headlights to shine at a slant through the vacant garage entryway. This would reveal signs of life while avoiding the most aggressive head-on approach. He meant to look like a concerned neighbor, not a suspicious busybody.

Stepping down from the cab, he laid his hand upon a medium-sized pipe wrench. He slid the tool along his forearm and up the sleeve of his heavy work shirt. Cradling the hook jaw against his palm, he was ready to drop and wield it on short notice. He had not fully rehearsed whether he meant to incapacitate the stranger then and there, or lure him into the truck with promises of hot meals. No God-fearing man should offer less to his unfortunate brother.

Something crashed beside his ear. He hadn't seen the beer bottle in flight, as his eyes were sorting shadows from light within the gutted shed. A fleck of glass rebounded off the wall, coming to rest just below the farmer's eye. He brushed it away with a baffled, instinctive motion, leaving a tiny scratch.

Now he saw the figure hunkered in the far corner, gathering more detritus to throw. Anger bloomed in the farmer's scrawny chest. Here was a drifter of no account or character, hurling garbage and stones before he knew friend from foe. A call to higher service would surely teach him.

"Steady, boy," the farmer said, aiming for a tone of gentle command. "I've come to offer a Christian hand, and a roof if you need it."

The spitting whelp moved fully into the light, and the farmer fell back with a faint gasp. The face before him was hard enough, wild-eyed, roasted by sun and tightened with defiant paranoia, but the illuminated body shrank to a fraction of what he had perceived at a distance. The rusty-golden curls of hair were not long and unkempt for a young man, but lopped off short for a female.

With a washed face and proper clothes on her, the girl might have been presentable to look at. As she advanced with a fistful of more jagged trash to throw, cussing incoherently as one might to scare off a dumb animal, she prompted only revulsion. Miles of road grit had sanded off any manners she'd been brought up to have.

"Fuck off! Fuck off me. Let me alone, y'old shitfuck!"

The olive jacket flapped loose on her, maybe once worn by a father or an older brother gone to war. It was hard to tell anything definite about her, except that drugs and broiling sun— maybe an unscrupulous trucker or two—had worked mischief on her. She was road-spoiled. Although she never could have guessed what the farmer had in mind by stopping, her distrust of all human contact was plain.

"See here now, young miss," he said.

"Get bent, cowshit bastard!" she yowled. "No business with you. Eat shit."

She backed like a crab against the wall behind her, eyes on the farmer's hand despite his attempts to hide it. He had let the wrench-head slip and poke from the sleeve cuff.

"Got no call," he said with a huff of anger, "young gal speakin' to an upstandin'—"

His head rang like an oily school bell and his vision went gray. The dirty girl-pup had thrown another bottle and struck his temple. He wavered back a step, his brain sending orders to swing his wrench and put the brat down. Instead, the signal got garbled, and he pissed about half his bladder.

She went crablike again, scuttling sidewise to get around him. In dizzy agony the farmer called on strength greater than his own to weave ahead of her, blocking her exit.

Truck.

The bitch-critter meant to break for his truck, to strand him while she drove off to some sordid destiny up the road. It could not be permitted.

Go, the traveler commanded, though the farmer could feel other wants pull at his brain stem. He would have liked to overpower the upstart, taught her hard lessons and found ways to make her sorry for her insolence.

Go, came the command again. *Others will come, and better.*

Gripping the door frame, the farmer planted the heel of his boot square at the bottom of the girl's ribcage. With a frantic reflex action, she grasped the boot with both hands, pulling it clean off his foot as he kicked her backwards. She landed hard, her breath hitching in little screams, and rolling over she soon began to cough and gag on dust.

The farmer could have taken her then, piled her into the truck and gone home vindicated, but the mere effort of opening his driver door nearly brought up vomit. He lacked the strength to wrestle with even a half-conscious body. He wished he could lock her inside, and see how she got along once the sun came up. Would she try to dig out through a dirt floor packed hard as granite, or slice herself up trying to crawl through a window frame?

If the farmer's kick had broken a rib, finding her wind again would not bring the girl much relief. The pain might compel her to lie there and cook, even without a door to shut on her. Nebraska sun was tough on folks who went by foot. For those with cracked ribcages, it might well be unbearable.

Never mind, he told himself before the traveler could speak again. The night was done, and let the devil take all memory of it. Others would come, and better. He swallowed the hard lesson in humility, and although he got sick twice on the way home, the taste of his own lively bile was a strange comfort.

It was after sunrise, not by much, when the truck sputtered

up the hardpack road toward the southeast farm gate. The final quarter mile ran through a disputed area between the farmer's land and that of his neighbor, Owens. Long ago, some crooked cousin of the Owens clan had held a minor county office, and he'd taken a foolish notion about access to mineral deposits practically on the fence line between the farms. He'd turned out to be as crazy as a nest of road lizards, but before his removal from office he'd engineered a knot of poorly drawn surveys and half-enforceable easements. Rather than wade those waters, the two landowners had made a handshake truce to share the land, which was only good for having a road run through it. Over nearly two decades, the men crossed that patch of dirt for daily chores and hardly set eyes on one another. A silent wave through a truck windshield had sufficed as greeting, an acknowledgment that peaceful relations continued.

The farmer was so unused to seeing a person on that road, let alone one on foot, he took the lanky shape for one of his homegrown hands that had blundered over the fence and lacked the wits to point itself back through the gate where it belonged. A trio of hated crows made a circling patrol above, as if they meant to dive at the walking figure for sport. Much as the farmer despised the airborne sickness, he braked to observe with grim curiosity.

Gunfire shattered the dawn quiet. The indistinct wanderer had raised a small shotgun, probably a .410, off its hip and blown the lowest bird from the sky. A harsh voice, cursing in clear English, followed the blast. The farmer had encountered a fellow human.

He knew Owens, the neighbor, as a specimen of bloated old age, nearly as broad as he was tall, and in poor health. His knees barely supported him, and he would not have ventured so far from his house except behind the wheel of a truck or tractor. Two sons lived around the place, neither of them much use except for loitering, spitting and smoking drugs out back of the stock tank where they thought themselves unobserved. The farmer had observed them. Even when slouching about they had the same gait and sandy hair as their old man in his more vital days.

The man before him, who turned to face the truck with his gun still half-raised, was someone else. He raised his chin in a wary greeting.

The gun put the farmer in mind of angry mobs. Perhaps this was merely the first of some local campaign against his operation, on the grounds of something his neighbors had found out or suspected about the last bountiful green field in the area. The farmer's foot twitched in expectation, needing only a quick drop of the accelerator to speed right over the armed man and settle his treacherous business. Then again, he had performed a virtuous crow-killing, not that the single casualty amounted to much.

Only as the man lowered the gun, and made an energetic summoning gesture, did the farmer recognize him. It was not a son, but the landowner's ferret-faced son-in-law, wed to the eldest daughter. She was as plain as a white pine floorboard, and about half as quick-witted. The farmer had dealt from time to time with this young man, who reckoned himself the heir apparent since the genuine offspring took no interest in manly work. He alone troubled the waters over the shared access road and other such petty matters, as though he already owned the farm for what little it was worth. He had a city education and spoke with corresponding smugness. The farmer had not been bothered by him lately, but his appearance typically meant trouble.

Rather than speak a proper greeting, the fellow muttered in his high-toned way, "So here you are, anyway." Arrogance issued from him like foul wind.

With a wrinkle of his nose, the farmer replied, "I come

around in my own time." He drew up a step or two shy of comfortable conversing distance. Aversion to the bad atmosphere between them was only part of it. The farmer wanted the perspective of one studying a pest insect, to see it at its full range of motion and predict its moves. Whether the younger man chose to interpret his reserve as the cold regard of an indifferent elder, or as cowed reluctance to engage, there were advantages either way.

"I suppose you'd concede," said the pup in his catalog-new flannel shirt and sickly wisps of mustache, "that this whole business is out of hand." He swung the shotgun barrel in a high arc to indicate the long-shadowed overgrowth of corn. "I can't say what sort of rotten dandelion weed you've bred with your crop to spring up in such tangles, but you'd need a circus of trained monkeys to pick any good corn from that mess."

"I reckon I get plenty good from it," the farmer spat back. The fog began clearing from his downtrodden mind.

The traveler, scornful of the farmer's diminishing ability, snacked on the mutual contempt hanging between them. The pup's ignorance, his disregard for all the farmer had wrought, carried the spicy savor of ghastly potential.

"Fact is, all you've done for yourself is breed a strain of aggressive crows that won't spook. You built a damned rookery nest for them, far as I can see. They're bound to eat up any decent output from your so-called rows."

"The odd scavenger flies through, I won't deny. Pecks an ear of my corn, though it pays in blood."

"Well, maybe you'd better raise your rates. They seem to be thriving, and any that you're driving off are straying across the property line. I'm catching them in our fields, our gardens."

The pup was not altogether wrong. The black-winged sickness was bothersome, and no small chore to keep down. In time, the farmer would have adequate help to protect his holdings. Not that he could share details with a stranger.

"I'm here to give you notice," the pup continued, swiveling his gun a fraction short of a threatening posture, "that me and mine on this land, we'll have no more of it. Fair warning, and more than you deserve, the second I'm back at the house I'm placing a call to the county. They'll take necessary measures, yes sir. See if they don't."

The farmer's skull vibrated with a grunt of disdain from the traveler. What swagger the pup had, so proud and protective of not-his-farm, not-his-land, the pitiful fruit of not-his-blood. He was a pretender to the claim on a dried-out shuck of a farm, unworthy even for the sickness to devour. For the sake of that he would call the authorities to dismantle the traveler's glory. If the scoffer could be made to see, how quickly he would worship and serve.

Resisting the urge to assert its authority on the spot, the traveler choked down its pride and guided its vessel to make a friendly overture. Better to lure all foes toward the heart, where it could marshal full power.

The farmer's head grew heavy, pushing him into a bow of sickening deference. Knowing the cost of resistance, he followed the cue and stammered in a docile tone. "It's fair warning, and I thank you for it, friend. Truth be told, maybe I'm out of my depth fighting the sick...them birds." His lips loosened, finding easier speech. "Listen, perhaps we never were friends but the g...good Lord made us neighbors. I reckon if the county comes in to smoke them critters out, they might have to do some encroachin' on your side also."

"We're willing to put up with what needs doing for the future good," said the pup. "Within reason."

"See, now," the farmer said, stepping forward to a friendly distance, flashing a sly grin almost wholly his own, "reasonable is one thing I've never known county men to be. I might have a plan to fix the birds and get my affairs back in order, without bothering you at all."

"Huh! That would be a fine trick."

"Fine indeed, friend," said the farmer, disregarding the insincere jab. Not so tricky as it seems, either, but I'd need a hand or two of help."

"I'm listening."

"I've got me a…a survey map back at home, would help me explain it. You're sharp enough to see it, only I'm not much for long explaining. Suppose you ride with me back to the farmhouse for a cup of decent coffee, and we'll see if we can't work out the fine points together."

The pup's face compressed. Clearly the thought of morning coffee with the farmer had no appeal, but he mastered his former rudeness. "I don't know if now's a good… I mean, the hour and…"

"Won't take more than half an hour to talk it out. My wife's about the place, of course, only she ain't inclined to add much to the talk. Might be I could find a drop of whiskey for our cups, if you'd rather." He pushed up a grin so guileless and chum-like that no sane man could sense danger in it, whether or not he took to the friendliness.

At last, the pup sighed. "Well, what's the harm?" he said. His obvious reluctance crumbled under the chance to school a rustic neighbor in property disputes, and to down a free belt of the man's liquor as he did so.

Bumping over the road through the main gate, the truck rippled with a mottle of green and black as morning sun crept through the jungle canopy of crops. The farmer's invited but unwelcome guest could not hide his amazement at the height and volume of corn seen from inside. He only lowered his gaze, with a pout of disgust, when streaks of guano painted the hood and windshield.

The farmer, at his master's bidding, kept up a fair line of questioning about the birds' incursion on the neighboring property, the pup's involvement with his in-laws' business, as well as his own ambitions for the place if he ever had a controlling say. After a few minutes of brief, hostile replies, the bottom line came through clearly.

"Listen, old timer," the pup snapped, "I'll sit a minute and look over your survey map or what have you, but make no mistake. I don't give a damn about your farm or your freaky crops. I only want to keep you from doing more damage, and rescue what I can from the ruin my wife's people have made of their holdings. I've got my own family to plan for. The sooner that farm is fixed up and off our hands, with the cash in the bank, the better. Understand? Does that satisfy you on my personal affairs?"

The traveler and the farmer smoldered with a shared contempt. No love of soil or work lay in this boy. The questions meant to probe his fitness as an apprentice had proved him unworthy. He was a common, craven auctioneer of respectable husbandry.

Rather than dwell on disappointment, the farmer drew his features taut in malefic satisfaction. There would be no need to call off the dozen scarecrows lurching in man-sized insect unison from the cornfield, obedient servants that gathered around the rusty farm truck as it slowed to a stop in the yard.

CHAPTER SEVEN

I'll Fly Away

The more she listened, the closer she came to changing her mind again. She sensed the danger of staying behind in the growing menace of her husband's shadow self. It would soon overtake all human trace of him. The slow return of her eyesight brought no reassurance. The wholesome familiarity of her beloved's face dissipated as she grew better able to look upon it.

The need for escape was urgent, and she would push her barely healed body as flight required. She had seen only a fraction of the monstrous tortures her husband visited on those he lured to the farm. From these glimpses alone, it was clear that no good fate awaited her. Part of her self-mastery involved training her ears to track his movements about the property. When he was away in the fields or in his truck—God knew where—out along the roads, she could know nothing of his activity. In the yard, in the house, and as far away as the barn, she followed his daily labors by the noise they made.

When he got on a tear out there, it might have been five men hammering away in that old loft, building some infernal combine. Whatever madness or evil gripped her lost husband, it had tempted the soul from him with blasted bushels of sweet juicy corn and promises of prosperity, replenishing some of the vitality in his wasted body. Even this could not explain the way he tricked her senses. One minute he seemed to tramp around the rancid kitchen, the next she heard him hauling lumber from his truck into the barn. An eye-blink later, he'd appear at her sickbed, asking with curt distraction after her health, a crock of his familiar sustaining gruel in hand.

Although not visibly grudging in his care of her, he was anxious. Perhaps reluctant to show affection, lest his resident demon judge him weak and deny him permission to visit her anymore. She might have preferred that, rather than see him grow so cold and strange. It was heartbreak enough to sense her own sanity slipping. She was barely able to separate one day from another.

Still, she could not submit. She must try to get away. He kept her alive and unharmed by the devils that troubled him, and for that she might have loved him through any extreme of agitation in lunacy or despair. But he was a murderer. She knew it for a certainty, and did not dare to forget it. If the shadow cloaking him was merely the mark of Cain, which in martyrdom she had been granted the power to perceive, it was enough to drive her out in hopes of dying someplace more safe. She could never find Paradise if he buried her in corrupt soil, compelling her body to nourish that farm of evil.

She practiced brief, halting trips from her bed, walking small circuits of the lightless room to make sure of her feet. At first she trembled like a foal at the knees, but her nerve and strength increased with the resolution that she would indeed go.

The second step was to beat her confusion and choose a moment when her husband would be farthest from home. She was too timid to try when she could hear him working in the barn. Although the racket kept his position fixed for her, he might stop at any moment, and if he saw her moving outside the house he could overtake her in a minute. Waiting until he left in the truck worried her almost as much, for she never knew when he might return, or from what direction. It seemed to her, though, that those mysterious errands took him off the farm for longer and longer spans of time. Whatever he went out hunting for, it grew either more scarce or harder to catch every time.

The clatter of tools from the barn subsided late the following morning. Shortly after, the truck's engine started and moved away across the property. The time had come for her to make haste in the opposite direction. Waiting was no longer safe.

She crept as quickly as she dared through the house, alert for new sounds. A rich rotten scent bloomed in her nostrils— the stewing of kernels in dark unnamable sludge on the stove. Her senses were too dulled by the familiar odor to put her guard up.

Even in the kitchen's poor light, she found her tender eyes a good deal more dazzled and afflicted than in her sickbed. She made her way to the center of the room, feeling for a table or chair to steady herself momentarily before striking out for the door and the yard beyond. Her hand settled on the smooth back slats of a chair her father had planed and joined by hand, another bolster to her courage. Despite her danger, she stroked its friendly curve, stopping short at a mass of squirming meat against her fingers.

Gasping, she reared backward, but not quickly enough to evade the face that twisted to meet her hand. The man in the chair—fully naked and bound to it—did not make sounds as a man ought to. Instead he formed the gurgling shrieks of a drowning thing. The clammy heat of fear in his wet exhalations bathed her palm. She shoved his mouth away, but he clamped spongy lips and gums onto her wrist, alternately gagging and suckling.

The man's teeth had been removed. His gullet brimmed with hot lumpy ooze, and she knew the feel of her husband's vile corn porridge between her fingers. The trussed victim was glutted, but kept trying to feed as if in fear of starvation.

Now she screamed, and a rough hand fell on her shoulder at the same moment. She'd known caresses from that hand, and strokes dealt in anger too. Her husband had been there in the house all the time, never mind what her maddened senses told her. Maybe someone else had been hammering in the barn and running the truck.

"Have you come in glad heart, woman?" thundered a voice she only half-knew. "To shoulder the burden and toil with us?" The black stew of corn and ichor dripped from a ladle in his hand. He had been feeding the wretched guest in the chair.

Her nostrils flared like an animal's in the slaughter pen. She did not need clear sight to know the raw textures of offal and blood underfoot. Since girlhood she had observed lamb and hog butchering, and there was no mistaking the slippery tendrils of gut as she trod on them in her panic.

She missed her chance to flinch away as he seized her hand, guiding it to the captive's chest and belly where crude sutures had sealed it up after disembowelment. Her fingers tensed at the give of soft flesh, the distended cavities lumpy with corn-muck. The woman had eaten of the same vile stuff, but not been sufficiently emptied of her human pieces to have her will extinguished. If her husband had bargained for her humanity as well as his own, she had little enough to thank him for. The farm clawed at her, even in her horror of it, while some strong part of her endured to tug, test and fray that bond.

The agonies of that degraded abomination in the chair told her what might soon happen to her. It had once been her neighbor, but it thrashed and whimpered as if ignorant of its uncanny rebirth. It no longer needed natural means to live. It was filled with the spirit of the farm.

Filled with the spirit, her inner voice repeated in a derisive croak.

She put all her limited might into twisting free, and her husband exclaimed in surprise as she broke his grip.

"Submit, woman," he said as if scolding a willful plow-horse. "We're at the end of our patience, and you're better suited to toil than to any more languishing."

She took a defiant step away from him, then another, but he didn't advance right away to stop her. "It's my fault frightening you with… all this business," he said. "You being laid up hurt so long, there's been no time to show you the glory of our work. But I'll teach you. You're not to serve in terror, but in love."

Now he took a step, but didn't close the distance between them as she continued moving.

"I've put them to work all over the farm," he said. "You'll see what marvels they are for dumb labor, and you can't tire them out. A gang of them's been helping me fix up the loft in the barn. That'll be the workshop, where I make more of them, and where I'll teach them to make more like themselves. I ought to have taken this pup there to finish changing him, only with you in bed I never thought of disturbing you, making this last one here in the kitchen. This house of ours will be for living in only, no darker business than that, if you'll stay and keep it with me."

She passed out the door. He ambled in her direction but didn't rush to pursue her, continuing his monotone sermon as though she weren't attempting to flee.

"I've arranged it all," he said. "Follow me, and you'll come to no more harm. We'll toil and serve together, just as we've always done, but no longer for our own fortunes. For the new plantings, and the greater harvest. Stop now, and you'll be spared."

The feel of open ground beneath her feet emboldened her. She cut straight away from the house toward the field before veering back again. She could not risk running into the old henhouse; her heart bounded like a rat in a soup can at the thought of crows biding their time there. She'd always believed birds were vicious things, likely to hold grudges. They could not know (and why should they care?) how her heart had changed against the farm. If once they caught her in the open, they would treat her as they had before, as they would treat anyone or anything that bore the farm's hateful stink.

The first rustle came in the shattered edge of her vision, an instant of dark motion among the rows. To her right, the vast outline of the barn told her she was more or less keeping a good heading for the road. Her stiff, pigeon-toed legs burned with sudden unaccustomed effort. Dizziness enveloped her. Specks of darkness gathered at the corners of her eyes.

Shapes continued to emerge from the corn, growing until she could make sense of them as figures running alongside her, keeping pace. Ragged forms of flannel and sacking, moving as clumsily as she but with far less effort in their speed. As they converged on her, she perceived them as no more than ghosts to be passed through. If she could break the bounds of the fearful apparitions, escape would lie shortly beyond.

Terror came an instant later as a different cluster of black rose from where it had sat, invisible to her, on the bare soil. A flock of crows, rising like a wall of Jericho. They had fooled her again, and she tumbled headlong as her legs gave out. Scooting backward, one arm thrust out to cover her eyes, she bleated in despair.

The first of the grisly scarecrows laid hands on her, pulling her to her feet. Rather than shrink in fright at its ghastly visage, the woman gave thanks that no bird had touched her first. The monster-men of dead meat and sodden straw, the helpers built by her husband to help in his unspeakable works, clustered around her. They jostled but did not bruise her as they marched her back across the yard to the doorway of the farmhouse. Her husband waited there, a curious determined expression on his face. He looked more like his old self than ever. Then, an instant later, he was less like his old self than ever. A voice rose, not from any throat, but from the earth below them.

"Come," it said, "and serve."

The farmer's outer aspect parted, and she saw his demon unmasked. At the sight, a sizable portion of her wits fled from her, never to return.

It would have been easier had she gone fully blind, or if her soul and that of her husband had been swallowed up entirely. No matter how fully the evil showed itself, she could see a remnant of her dear one trapped inside. Every fiber of her body and mind shouted to leave the poor fool in the hell he had invented, all but the final courage needed to move her toward flight again. She stayed, and she lived alongside him, finding solace in the world not as it was but as her devastated mind recalled it.

The pageantry of her old chores, even those no longer needed, preserved her sense of belonging on the homestead. She sewed and tailored, gathered and cooked, hummed sweet old tunes around the house and the barn. Steering wide of bird and scarecrow alike brought a measure of peace. Her heart ceased to chide her when she mistook one perfectly common and plain thing for another. The farmer even fixed up a semblance of her old milking stool, and a sham effigy of the cow stuffed with husks and rubbish.

She kept her husband's human remnant warm, trying time and again to till the seeds he planted in her. Soon, the grief attending persistent failure came no more. Letting the hard-won sharpness of her faculties decline, allowing her sense of things to go dim and cobweb-soft, eased all pains without bias.

CHAPTER EIGHT

Just As I Am

The traveler walked its domain, surveying the fields and the silent, somber hands at work in them. Months passed in the world beyond the fence, yet on the farm a single growing season continued. Crops were collected in their due time, carted to the cribs and the barn loft for their appointed uses, and to keep them from the ravenous beaks of the bird-vermin. Still, there came no Great Harvest, the time promised in the shredded fibers of the traveler's memory, from the bygone age when it had set out with definite plans to take root and spread its influence. The goal and intention of its dreadful pilgrimage was lost in swirls of green shoots, veined with black.

The dark-winged sickness made constant incursions. A vanguard of scarecrows patrolled the fields to repel fresh attacks, while the others gathered corn and stood ready to make more of their own kind in the barn.

After converting the neighbor fool and pressing him into service, the farmer honored his promise not to make another one in the house. Even so, he still supplied most of the fresh bodies for the process. Only once in a while would a scarecrow catch and subdue a hapless trespasser by itself. The farmer's creations were drones, better suited to simple, clear and repetitive tasks than to improvised action.

Fearing inquiries after the neighbor's disappearance, the farmer had wasted no time inviting Owens and his two other sons to the farm. For pretext he requested their help mending a fallen joist in the barn, and promised a manly toast with his own special home-brew. Once he had them inside the barn doors, unarmed and unsuspecting, he had allowed his scarccrows to wclcomc and initiatc thcm.

As the farmer had suspected, no further friends or concerned relations came to him seeking the inhabitants of the

Owens farm. All who had come to the farm now served. None had resisted with any power or authority.

As for the birds, they were only birds. Malformed, fertile and constantly annoying, they could do no more than pester and peck.

The traveler was slow to admit a more insidious worry. It had waited too long, been too exacting in its expectations for a successor. The farmer was used up, another vessel needed without question. The stagnant operation had to be taken in hand with fresh, bloody vigor. It was not a sick old man's task, nor one fit for common vagrants or the weak-willed young. To annex and overgrow more land would take sharp wits and powerful hands. How could the traveler have guessed that after latching onto its only choice of host, a farmer on the brink of death by his own hand, no worthier candidate would happen by? Truly it was a desolate place the traveler had chosen to settle.

If only the paltry soil of the woman could nurture the feeble seed of the man, an heir would even then be ripening for its birthright. The traveler craved a strong young body to carry it, but none except the farmer carried an inborn devotion to the home soil. Fed only on corn, riddled with mites and pellagra together with a dozen other earthly frailties, the farmer and his hardship-demented wife were well into their physical decline. The traveler could not restore them to health or prolong their lives indefinitely. If doom lay in remaining bound to the farmer, was it foolish to dream of recruiting a worthy inheritor?

To journey so far before taking root had been a mistake. Run to its extreme limit of energy, the traveler had fastened itself to a host barely in time. On first inhabiting the farmer it had perceived an ideal combination of able body, troubled spirit and malleable will, much as a starving desert creature might savor any old carcass or brackish puddle as pure, hearty food.

The parts of its being connected to previous forms in its life cycle had degenerated to feed its new bond to the farm. It had only inchoate recollections of a master force commanding it to walk as far as it could, take deep root where it stopped, and consume all that came within its reach. Others of its kind had wandered in every direction, obeying the same command. Some would nest in coastal wetlands, others in snowy mountain passes. Hitching a ride on the small airplane had been a spontaneous decision, an attempt to travel a few hundred miles beyond its natural endurance. Back then, perhaps it had hoped for some extra reward or approbation from its now-forgotten master. It was the sort of reckless action that pious humans took to please their deities. The traveler had learned that from the decomposing minds of the farmer and his wife. It had also learned what humans feared above all else - ravaging cancers that ate their healthy tissues and stole their allotted years on the perishing planet.

The traveler clung, having no alternative, to a strained faith in some future incarnation. If it could only outlast and abide a while longer, it would find stronger and stronger hosts to inhabit than the brittle, decrepit shell housing it now. The farmer would soon be too crippled to roam the county roads in his ailing truck. The scarecrows needed a master of sound body and mind.

Sensing his own obsolete condition, the farmer became increasingly reclusive alongside his woman. The traveler permitted it. Let them wall themselves up in the farmhouse. Dormancy, even in a chrysalis of malnourished squalor and torment, would help preserve whatever diluted essence remained. The future might call for strength, as much as the poor host could summon.

The scarecrows were hardy enough, able to feed themselves on the new corn they gathered and repel the sickness. The problem of the birds remained a tolerable but constant nuisance. Their wings came away with a pull from sinewy arms. Their nests littered the soil in the deepest recesses of the cornfield, under the eaves of any standing structure and even a number of small burrows along the fence. Many of them were hardly birds at all anymore, yet their eggs were as fragile as ever, easy to stomp and smash. Let their feathered corpses and the yolks of their unhatched young provide what fertilizer might ooze from them.

The farm grew on, unbothered, hidden in plain sight from all but a few. The outward calm of hibernation sheltered the frenzy of activity within its boundaries. The place drew silently into itself, for all the world like a dormant wasp nest, needing only the proper disturbance to tear it back open and alert the traveler that a glorious change, so long awaited, so keenly suffered for, had come to pass.

PART THREE: FOR DUST THOU ART

(LAST NIGHT)

CHAPTER ONE

Not Alone Anymore

The shock of horrified grief dulled JT's first impressions of being brought inside the farmhouse. In a more collected state, he might have put up a better fight, though the combined strength of that many scarecrows could have broken him in several places by the time he shook them off.

One of the creatures had shown the primitive sense and initiative to pick up JT's gun when they took him. The farmer accepted it from the scarecrow with an appreciative leer. JT could not recall whether he'd reloaded after his final shot in the cornfield.

They ran a mighty fast operation on the ol' farm that time forgot. Bobby and Lisa had been taken, somehow, and turned into replicas of those monsters in a matter of hours. JT spent more time reflecting on this than consciously observing as they hustled him into the musty, lamp-lit kitchen and yanked his hands and feet in four separate directions. Medieval torture, at least the kind seen in old Hammer horror movies, was the first thing to cross his mind at being spread apart and fastened to some object in the room. He preferred to think of inquisition scenes rather than contemplate the potential warmup to a Cornhusker gangbang.

Whatever their plans, virgin sacrifice was the least likely goal. JT had hard miles on him, and his bitter high-test blood wouldn't appease any gods.

Trying to unflex, he found himself bound to a short wooden chair, low-backed enough to fit a well-grown child. His arms were pulled down parallel in back. Sharp twists of fence wire fixed his wrists to the rear legs under the seat, and his ankles to the front legs. JT's fingers danced like pinned insects, trying to find the ends of their bonds, but proved too stubby and awkwardly cocked to gain purchase. His aching spine bent a few degrees backward over the top of the chair, thrusting his chest up and forward. His neck muscles quivered with painful fatigue in any position. The rattle of his own breath astonished him; it might have been the distant noise of some broken farming machine.

The chair appeared to be the only intact furniture in the house. A lopsided table stood on two good legs and one that was nearly broken off where it joined the top. A crooked basin was nailed beneath a pump against the wall, but over its edges dripped a substance too dark and thick for well water. The squat stove, which must long ago have devoured the rest of the wood furnishings and floorboards, glowed from its belly with serene, sinister hunger.

Scanning for more in the weak sputter of grimy lanterns, he barely registered the other human form tied with rags and twine in a slumped vertical posture against the wall, where a sizable hole exposed a few feet of bare timber. It was a young woman, her drawn face vaguely familiar to JT, but never until she gasped with unexpected signs of life would he have known her for his wife. In his life he'd seen the physical impact of shock and stress on a lesser scale, but Katy might have undergone a week of starvation and rough treatment from her used-up look since their capture by cornfield monsters. It didn't occur to him until later that he might be reduced to the same living corpse pallor.

Something squatted near his knees, examining him from below. It was a woman, or had been, her vacant face ensnared by a nest of filthy hair. She was barely distinguishable from one the farm's creatures in burlap and bloody overalls. Her gingham and homespun rags gave a clue to her identity, even with the distracting detail of the knife she wielded alongside her idiot grin, half-poised to stab JT's belly should he make a false twitch.

This dark spoof of Puritan modesty, JT thought, could only

be the farmer's wife. Not any farmer's wife but the archetype of the idea. Judging by her state of ruin, she belonged in a set with this mad farmer whose land had fallen into hellish chaos. Who had so angered Big Bad Mama Nature as to pervert the common crow, now repurposed and deployed as an avian dirty bomb against its further growth. A farmer who'd cooked up a way to vanish ordinary folks and set them loose again as slave-things that never should walk free or be seen by the sun.

The farmer appeared in JT's limited view, staring with a kind of twisted plea in his sunken eyes. The shadow he cast was unnaturally dark and rigid on the wall, given the room's nearly lightless conditions. The darkness at the farmer's heels put all the room's other dark spots to shame. JT's throat tightened with revulsion. His mind focused all the anger and fear that had colored the previous day to an arrowhead point. He imagined drawing a bow at twenty yards and firing his misery into the bloodless, ravaged boot-sole of a face that studied him nose-to-nose for… What could it possibly want?

As if hearing his thought, the farmer spoke. "Time's near, son. And let the children rejoice."

JT spat, partly from rage but also because his mouth was full of blood from a split lip. "Rejoice?" he said. "I'll rejoice you all the way from Sunday to motherlovin' doomsday, you chicken-fried psycho. What the fuck do you want from us?"

The farmer blinked, not as fazed by JT's display as JT might have hoped. "You'll learn the ways. I've been a poor vessel, but faithful. Hard seasons, holdin' out against them birds, me and the wife. But those others we built, to toil and grow, they'll abide and serve at your word when I've took my leave."

JT didn't allow the soft answer to dissuade him. "What the shitfire are you spouting, you old fool? Whatever's here, this thing you call a farm doesn't deserve to stand another moment. Do the world a favor, burn this house down and yourselves in it. I'll be taking my wife and going. You let me up now, and I won't beat you to death." He laid it on bitterly, unmindful of his vulnerable position, in the hope of rattling somebody's nerves besides his own. A gentle push might be enough to unseat the farmer's temper. It must be fragile, given the holy-spitting maniac he seemed to be.

The farmer pointed a shaky, admonishing finger. "Spirit's a fine thing, and it'll serve you plenty. But you'll not be so high or mighty when the time comes. He'll create in you something more than you've ever been. Don't make it hard on us both."

"What time? Who'll create what? You took my only brother and made him a by-God abomination, you chicken-plucking waste of air."

"Now, fair's fair. What I and mine did was mold your brother to better use. Wasn't me who put him down with a scattergun." The farmer's voice rippled with menace, almost amusement, at getting one over on a raving stranger.

JT let the comment burn in his guts for exactly one second before he resumed his litany of top-volume obscenities. He paused every few seconds to shout at Katy, hoping to rouse her. All the while, the edges of the farmer's shadow danced and pooled around him, like scummy pond water drizzled with rain.

Rather than spring to her husband's defense at JT's onslaught, the farmer's wife yelped and scrambled away on all fours, never mind her advantageous possession of a knife. Once clear of him, she rose to her feet and slouched away toward where Katy sat. JT watched the woman and hoped she would not stab or slash Katy in a show of dominance. He thought he saw Katy draw a quick breath and hold it. Perhaps she'd bruised a rib and couldn't breathe without some degree of pain. They'd have to take the first opportunity to break their bonds and overpower their captors, then assess how badly they'd been hobbled or slowed against escape.

JT hoped that if all chance of a getaway was lost, they'd brain him quickly before they tried skinning his face off, or fed him some of his own brother with grits and eggs. His stomach made a ghoulish rumble at the mental picture of hot breakfast. The rush of hunger was a mutiny of his body against his wits, and the nausea that followed knocked the gallows humor out of him. Bobby was long gone, he knew, his ordeal over and his remains more than likely recycled or thrown into the corn for fertilizer. JT's imagination calibrated to a new perspective on whatever horror story had him and Katy in its clutches now.

The farmer's wife shuffled around the room in erratic loops, caterwauling without sense, brandishing her beat-to-hell kitchen knife like a protective amulet. She scarcely seemed aware or interested in where she was, or who was there with her.

JT did not take advantage of the feeble-minded as a rule, but she was the most pliant variable in his line of sight. Coiling his legs as tightly as possible, he sprang in her direction and managed to bring his weight and the chair down across her startled body. She wriggled and wailed beneath him like a gutshot rabbit, the fist holding the knife twitching dangerously close to JT's eyes. He ground an elbow and a knee into her soft parts, answering her cries with menacing growls. To his surprise, she went still and quiet.

"Yeah," JT muttered, "how 'bout everybody quits waving knives and we all calm down, huh?"

The farmer hopped from foot to foot, advancing to defend his wife only to be drawn back by the force that held him. "Get off, boy," he said through withered lips. "You turn my wife loose. Off her, hear? Else we'll make it hard on ya."

JT turned the flat of the blade with his chin, positioning it so the dented point pressed against thin flesh near the top of his throat. The farmer's wife quivered but did not move, afraid to push or pull her weapon across JT's throat in self-defense.

Not afraid of JT, clearly, but reluctant to take executive action on her own.

"Get *off*," came the command again, with new strength and a deeper resonance.

JT did not pull his neck out of danger. "Kill me, you chickenshit loony! Get your kicks off someone who'll take your nonsense with a straight face. Put me in the combine, stack me in the corn crib, thresh me into whatever scumbag zombie turns your crank, and be done with it quick or so help me, I'll cut my own throat and spoil your fun right here. I'm the last company you'll have for a while, so carve me up good. You have no power over me if I take it from you, worthless daddy-humping crowbait hayseed."

He raved on in less and less coherent fashion, putting all attention on himself so Katy might not come to harm. If he could convince the farmer he was suicidal and wouldn't give the satisfaction of begging for life, he wouldn't exactly be holding an ace, but a wild card was just as good.

The farmer's untethered shadow raised itself to greater height and substance. Tendrils like tar played over the man's crusted work clothes, forcing the curved spine straight and rearing the old sodbuster up to the posture of a younger, more vigorous man. He did not tower, exactly, but he loomed, and his voice descended into a doom-filled rumble. JT faced a separate and larger entity than the decrepit old farmer, one which used the withered vessel as a dummy mouthpiece for its own private reasons.

"Silence, pilgrim! There is life left to you yet. Life, and choices. Be still and pay heed."

JT held still, but he didn't shut up to pay heed. "How do you reckon we've got choices? This looks like every murder hole I ever saw in a crummy B-movie, only uglier. What choices do we have here except how quick we check out?"

"Are you not still alive? You have not been taken to the

barn. If it had been appointed, you would have beheld the altar by now. Let that be covenant enough." The voice had fully transformed now, replacing the reedy slur with a thunderclap, flowing up through the farmer but no longer spoken by him. The living cloak of shadow clenched around the knobby throat, knees, and elbows, cradling the farmer but also shaking him like a hoodoo stick.

"My..." JT gasped, and checked himself. Besides the shame of his part in how Bobby had ended up, speaking the word "brother" to whatever he was addressing seemed indecent. "The ones who came yesterday... Why not keep them alive too, like us?"

The doom voice came again. "They were as children, peering at windows. Fit only to serve."

"And we... I'm not fit for that?"

"In you we see more. A master of the land." The spindly thing working the farmer as its puppet became plainer, creeping over the gritty earth in his direction. "You who brought such an offering of strong new flesh across the barren outskirts, into this thriving fertile sanctuary. You who weathered the pestilence of black wings. A hardy pilgrim, to be sure."

"Pestilence? What, those fat mean-ass crows? To hell with those ugly things. They're what drove us to this dirty cornhole."

A wet chuckle slid like oily chains up from the farmer's belly. "Fool shit crows. They're a sickness to more than the farm. The countryside is blighted with them."

JT considered his perspective on the whole mess. Dreadful as the crows were, breaking nature's barriers to spread like locusts and terrorize the locals, they were doing their best to eat up the foul farm's yield. There may have been a time when they'd come— or been sent—to pull up a bad root which had poisoned the acreage. If there was a good side to the mayhem that had swallowed JT and his family, this gave him a clear plan for when the time came to choose allies. Disgusting as they were, JT would cast his lot with those goiter-dragging mite-ridden birds, no question. The farm team of broken humans, former humans and subhumans appealed far less to him.

The farmer's body jerked and danced, joints creaking, like a doll shaken by some frustrated thing that wanted stronger toys to play with.

Seeing that display shifted JT's innards again. Bracing his will against the fear of pain, he lowered his chin against the knife point until the skin broke and warm blood flowed. Beneath him, the farmer's wife had stopped whimpering, and fluttered against him with quick heartbeat and shallow breaths. She lay as if in mortal fear of moving without permission.

JT pushed away thoughts of the untold filth and rust leaching off the knife blade into his bloodstream. He hoped the thin curtain of red running down his throat made a convincing signal of his determination.

"What happens to your little party if I keep falling on this knife?" he asked, every syllable stinging.

"You will be stopped in time." The doom voice appeared to have regained its control, but did JT detect a hint of a tremor? "You will not be released to death but will serve. And first, you will see her…your woman…made like them." The farmer's listless arm gestured to Katy, who drew another labored breath.

JT had no need to wonder, *Made like who?* It was obvious who "them" was. The farm had one career path for living humans who blundered too near—gutted, stuffed, and scarecrowed. Who knew how many souls had been captured and mutilated into half-rotten drones? Tend the rows, fight the crows. Whenever they decided they'd grown enough, there would be one hell of a harvest festival in town again.

There were exceptions, at least two he could think of. That farmer, possessed or cocooned or whatever, bore a strain of human consciousness which could be pushed into use when it suited the doom voice that called the shots. The farmer's wife was the saddest of all. Her brittle thinness under his elbow told a tale of suffering. In her place, who wouldn't go as crazy as a bedbug circus? She may have been the farm's only fully human resident for years. Neither she nor her husband were young, to say nothing of crippling malnutrition. The corruption of the farm was dug into them.

The farmer's body hunched forward expectantly. JT thought of spitting in his eye, but softened his voice almost to politeness. "Master of the land," he said. "You…want a new boss for this place. You've worn out your old skin." There was no point in being tactful. The farmer was hardly present.

"Master, yes," the doom voice said. "Heir to all you survey. Alone you are lord of nothing, but with our help…"

Sure, JT told himself. *Help like a creeper vine to a tree, until it strangles the poor fucker.*

He held a suspenseful silence as long as he could, tilting his head to draw fresh drops from the wound in his chin. Painful pressure kept him alert, and if he could intimidate or impress his captors at all, taking more pain might be the best way to do it. He thought the farmer's wife must have fainted beneath him.

The air outlining the farmer began to boil and fuzz. He looked like a worn-out videotape image with a tracking problem. In revealing itself more fully to JT, the creature showed its desperation. It laid itself open to him, waiting to infest. Its dominion had slipped for who could say how long. JT doubted that a hard-headed mortal so-and-so like himself could outlast the patience of such a being, even a dying one, before he grew too exhausted or hungry to resist.

"What about Katy?" he asked. "You told me…if I tried to kill myself. But wouldn't you just make her one of…those…anyway?" Intoning Katy's name in his negotiation drove a nail of ice through his heart. Her name was the only good thing his lips might ever speak again.

The doom voice answered in its own voice, as well as the farmer's, with dreadful dignity. "And he who kept the garden cried unto the Lord, saying, Master I am troubled for the sake of Thy fruits. Lo, who is more subtle than the gore-crow that seeketh to corrupt the harvest? And the Lord did fashion from the thriving crop a legion of helpmates to ease their toil and rend the sickness asunder."

JT was no Bible scholar, but the doom voice took its text from some cockeyed warp of what he recalled being preached at him in his youth.

"You'd… spare her?" JT ventured. "To be my wife and live with me here while I took over… What the hell would I be taking over, anyway?"

"What hell indeed?"

"No, I mean…all this mopey sermon-making and I don't have the first damn clue what all this is for. This crummy farm…all that guano-blasted corn, to feed what?"

The room rumbled with suppressed outrage. "You dare blaspheme the splendor of what we have sown?"

"I dare, bucko. Give me one sensible reason to take this promotion, and I'm your company man."

A silence fell. JT had expected old Corn-thulhu to have a quick answer for everything, but it rumbled and fumed as if he'd thrown its logic with the simplest question. Rational human perspective no longer figured in its calculations, if it ever had.

"You…" the doom voice offered with only a fraction of hesitation. "You shall sow sons upon the woman, to rule this dominion after you. A legacy, unlike the poor unworthy vessels who have kept their vigil before you."

There it was: a dynasty of farmers, breeding overseers to run their legion of brainless devils. The human element was important to whatever called the tune on the farm, but one busted-up old couple was never meant to run it alone. The doom voice had counted on more humans with the pride of the land born into them, but…what? Couldn't get its cornstalk up?

Abandoning their bid for natural children by the farmer and wife, the powers that rotted were pushing for an urgent religious conversion – his – to start the bloodline over. JT and Katy had danced ineptly around the topic of having kids since before their marriage, but while each believed in the other as a fine potential parent, neither had the same faith in their own aptitude for it.

Lisa… Dear God…

Lisa and Bobby might have taken to it differently. The grim almost-certainty that once their vacation was over, Bobby's next adventure would be to deal with the prospect of an imminent baby, hurt JT's heart so much he could barely stand to think it. Bobby and Lisa would have been beautiful parents. JT had thought it before, even mentioned it to Katy once or twice, and they agreed it just fit.

Even so, there was enough hereditary evidence on JT's side to make his mouth dry up at the prospect of fatherhood. He knew he'd accept the job, presented with a child of his own who had slipped past the usual precautions, but would he take it on deliberately even in the best of circumstances? Here it would be cult-daddy pageantry, condemning their barefoot brats to inherit a tract of land whose nature he dreaded to ponder. An offer to rule over hell and multiply should have presented a hell with more sex appeal. Some gig it promised to be, working off another man's contract with the unholy. Could he allow any natural son or daughter of his to be born for that?

His thoughts drifted featherlike back to Katy—the love of

his life. If his cooperation gave her a chance of surviving the night and escaping that foul house intact, what could he do but agree? If he let whatever spoke in the doom voice enter him, could it ever be held in check or vomited out? What sort of control would be left to him, not as an old shell as the farmer had become but with his young strength and obstinate mindset? Could he and Katy find a way to exorcize it together, or die trying?

The farm woman squirmed into consciousness beneath him, with a tentative "Ehhhh?" he took for asking to be let up. He weighed the horror of seeing Katy turned scarecrow against the possibility of seeing her come to the same pathetic state in the role of farmer's wife. He credited Katy with saving his soul, however true that was, and to risk sending her down the path of that doddering lunatic, too aware of her damnation not to go stark jabbering crazy, was the greater abomination. The crows in their blind, all-destroying way had it right. The farm was the worst of all present evils.

"No sale, Jethro," said JT, and pushed himself down against the knife point to see how hard he could prick his captor's anxiety.

A warbling howl shook the farmhouse as JT's mouth spread in a petulant smile. He half-expected the farmer to keel over dead, his handler oozing away to an inconsequential stain. Instead, he gasped as bony gloved hands wrenched him upward by the hair. A small gang of scarecrows, which must have lurked in the doorway awaiting their master's word, had limped over. The biggest had grabbed JT, nearly scalping him with its violent pull.

A second scarecrow lifted the farmer's wife from her prone position and set her on her feet. She scampered to the corner where Katy still slumped against her restraints. Katy's eyes were shut, and her breathing was so shallow that JT could not be sure whether he truly saw it or not.

Now JT realized that he might have miscalculated. In his talk with the farmer and the doom voice, he had forgotten the scarecrows. They occupied the farm in such numbers that without some greater strike at their vital source, the devil's hex that allowed them to run on tainted corn distillates in a mindless but useful state of living death, they could overpower any resistance.

Before he could frame another complete thought, the grimy shadow rode the farmer across the room in four long strides. JT looked away, as much as his racked position allowed, from the old man's probing eyes which had turned a glossy green-black. Dry lips parted with a series of soft noises, as if the farmer were preparing to take a hungry bite of his cheek. Then, when the wasted shoulders hitched in quiet contractions, JT understood what was about to happen with a scorch of panic in his belly. He had seen some version of this performance a thousand times, by the dozen stray cats he and Katy had fed and fostered; the farmer was getting ready to disgorge…something… And it was aiming for JT.

He thrashed, trying to keep from puking on himself, as ancient bile smells wafted from the farmer's withered mouth into his nose.

Katy released a lungful of air that she'd been holding for more than a minute, and sagged against the wall. Her bindings were looser than moments ago. She'd had the presence of mind to hold her breath while they tied her up, then put regular stress on the decaying scraps they'd used to do it. Now she seemed almost able to wiggle free, her bonds making little rips as she thrashed from side to side.

The farmer's wife spied her and started a round of her

frantic sing-song complaints. Katy did not pause to consider the woman's potential to change allegiance in this madhouse, if by some argument she could be persuaded to help. Katy had seconds to stop her from alerting others that a captive would soon be loose and on the run.

"Shut up," she said. "Just back off." When the woman wouldn't be quiet, Katy lost her temper and kicked. Her foot connected with a shin like a dry branch, and the woman responded with a series of wild stabs at the would-be escapee.

Katy hissed as the crooked knife punctured her upper arm near the shoulder. The wound wasn't deep but it hurt plenty, dialing her adrenaline up another few notches. Her shabby bonds broke a few seconds later.

Now that her blood was up, Katy felt brave enough to charge the farmer-thing which was occupied with the task of retching on JT, but the farmer's wife had not stopped in her efforts to cut and maim. She flew at Katy, her knife hand chopping swaths of air at chin level.

Katy fell back on wobbly legs. Feeling along the wall, she discovered a door frame almost invisible in the poor light. The door hung crooked and would not take much more force before it splintered off its hinges. Unlike the house's other wooden fixtures, it had not been chopped apart for stove wood, leading Katy to suspect that it still served an important function. If any kind of refuge or secret place lay beyond, it might give Katy a chance to regroup and strike back at whatever barred their hasty exit. She'd been too focused on regulating her breath in the noxious air of the kitchen to fully grasp what was happening with JT, but he'd have to hold out a few minutes longer.

A shard of JT's consciousness witnessed Katy's act of self-liberation. He wondered where in that soiled hell she could have gone, and how soon she'd be back for him.

A thick tar-like slop hit the bridge of his nose. It smelled of stomach acid and ethanol, bubbling from the farmer's wattled gullet and oozing with nasty slowness over JTs face. Full of grit and silt, it ran in streaks across his chin and forehead. JT forced his eyes and mouth shut. He blew harsh puffs from both nostrils, determined to keep everything out. For a while, it worked. Eventually his twitching eyelid let him down. The substance did not cause immediate pain, but his lid and eyeball prickled the way his foot might when he'd sat on it for too long. Although the sensation was anything but comfortable, JT did not dare cry out for fear of having even a droplet run down his throat.

As the tingle settled, the burning arrived, and JT was alarmed to find himself seeing out of the shut eye. Indistinct images ran like scenes on a worn filmstrip. Rather than seeing, exactly, he was being shown something. Long ago he'd worked security at a self-storage compound outside Shreveport, and the shifting visual input reminded him of watching a monitor cycle through its multi-camera feed.

All moving things claimed by the farm glowed from within, not quite infrared images but similar. The farmer's head was a dull ember, the effluent he spouted a brilliant flood of purple and green compared to the swampy lusterless crap it looked like to a healthy human eye. The undulating shape behind, under and around the farmer—the word *traveler* appeared uninvited in JT's mind—glowed with the same livid tones as the vomited muck. As more and more of the stuff dripped onto his face, chest, and hands, JT felt heavy pressure on him as though it were straining to penetrate his outer layers.

He did not manage to repel pollution as completely as he'd have liked. Stray drops and dabs found their way into him, seeping through the nicks and cuts he'd recently picked up. The thundering disembodied doom voice – the voice of this "traveler," he supposed – talked more clearly and insistently in his mind now.

Grow, surrender. Welcome the traveler, submit and grow. For the harvest. Sons upon the land. For her. Grow and serve. No death. Grow and serve, above or below. Grow.

All JT could do was resist. No one else could hear. No one could come to his aid, until Katy returned.

The vision from his tainted eye left the room, soaring over the farmyard and out above the rows. What JT saw was hopelessness. The property teemed with scarecrows on patrol—tending the corn, fetching tools, cutting and binding stalks, carrying sheaves, all of them surely ready to snatch up anything that fled past them. Each of them glowed with a dimmer light than the traveler's, but it was made of the same substance. The flourishing stands of corn gave off that horrible radiance as well. The crows were easy to discern, but only in contrast. They appeared as tiny negative spaces, flitting black holes in the film that played against his optic nerve. They tangled with the shining scarecrow dots, their tireless combat never pausing for more than a few seconds.

Seeing it all as the farmer saw it—as the traveler meant to make him see it— JT comprehended the magnitude of the danger surrounding them. He reflected again that if only he could know what powered the farm in its rotting trance of death...

As the thought of it crossed his mind, the clarity of his vision enhanced. Perhaps if he'd let the farmer feed him, swallowed the traveler's repellent essence willingly, he might have received a blissful epiphany that overwhelmed and seduced him to the side of the farm. There was a magnificence to its ghastly scale, but nobody with a shred of their human will intact could kneel in service to it. The traveler, whatever it was and whatever had set it loose on the world, imbued the soil with its unholy properties. The corn that grew in the soil filled the bellies of the undead scarecrows with nasty vital force. A portion of the traveler infected and governed the farmer, while another large and powerful piece must be resting somewhere it could nurse and grow the corn, undisturbed by chance discovery or interference.

He saw it, only for an instant. A twisted root, in the shape of an elongated corpse with pulsing black tendrils extruded from its limbs, lay at the junction of earth and water in the bottom of the well. There it was safe to pump like a diseased heart into the poisoned breast of the farmland.

JT thought he could find it without much trouble, if he could get outside. The next question was impossible to answer just then: could he get there soon enough?

The kitchen had been a stripped-bare chamber of horrors, but was cozy compared to the yawning lightless place in which Katy found herself. For the handful of seconds it took for her pupils to adjust, the far wall seemed not to exist. If it had turned out to be the mouth of a pit leading underground, Katy would have believed it. By slow degrees, her straining eyesight filled in the dimensions of an ordinary vacant room.

It only seemed cavernous on account of being so empty. The absence of floorboards, burned long ago or used to blockade windows, heightened the effect even more than it had in the kitchen. It also ruled out her hope for a trapdoor leading to a secret cellar. In the relative quiet Katy could better hear the constant, stormy beat of wings from the yard outside. and the occasional peck of malicious beaks against the siding. That sound alone, over a period of weeks or months, would have been enough to drive any farmer and wife walleyed crazy. Never mind how sick they'd been to begin with. Katy was compassionate beyond the average measure, but her heartstrings were more tuned to physical suffering. She despised it, but she could comprehend it. Diseases of the mind and soul frightened her far too much to trigger her tenderness easily.

She followed the line of the nearest wall to the corner, with no idea how much time she had before the farmer's wife or something worse came groping after her. She hoped to stumble on a loose piece of debris, maybe a discarded scrap of furniture, that she could use as a weapon.

A right-angle turn at the corner brought her to the opening of a passage, about the width of a cattle chute, formed by an inner wall constructed parallel to the wall she'd been following. It had not been visible from where she'd entered, and Katy felt ill at the thought of pressing further into the house's hidden spaces, but she knew what was behind her and meant to explore every alternative.

She stumbled over something just after her second turn, where the confines of the passage opened again. A small mound of earth, no larger than the foot that kicked it, caught her toe and pitched her forward onto her outstretched palms. Her muscles coiled, ready to spring her up onto her feet again as she would have done after a lively set of push-ups, but she spotted several more tiny hills in the dirt.

It was a miniature cemetery. The disturbances were unmarked graves, half a dozen in all, each barely big enough to hold a rodent or small bird. None of them, certainly, could have housed the remains of a healthy newborn human.

The tiny desolate memorial brought Katy close to fainting under a sudden surge of her feelings. She could have sat down and wept with grief for the miserable mother, who had taken such pains to bury her little ones in this hollow of damnation, if minutes before she hadn't been fleeing in mortal dread of the vacant-eyed monster the farm had made of that mother.

Katy found a more sympathetic proxy for her sorrow. Her heart ached for poor sweet Lisa, whose future hadn't even presented itself. All for a good time, a proper introduction to the family, she'd come west and been cast into hell's corn-clogged throat. A young woman ready to grab life and taste it, with untold successes in her path, Lisa had instead become a blood offering to the wasteland. Vanity, vanity, more than one religious authority had intoned in Katy's youth. All of it vanity. In that moment, continuing her search of the room while nearly blinded by hot grieving tears for Lisa and Bobby and their snuffed possibilities, she came as close to understanding that dire quotation as ever before in her life.

She stood in an ankle-high pile of dried corn husks. There was no getting away from them around here. The rustle and crackle underfoot turned her stomach, especially once she realized they had been gathered into a sort of nest. Their dusty aroma mingled with a richer, all-too-human musk. She supposed that when and if the farmer and his wife slept, this pallet served as their bedding. Perhaps the babies buried in the far corner had been conceived here, once the couple had burned their bedstead for fuel.

Her shuffling foot kicked against a new obstacle. Something made of plastic and metal clattered aside, and a small square of hard silver-blue light glowed on the floor. Having seen nothing but dirty lanterns, candles, and starlight for hours, Katy blinked in momentary confusion at a battery-powered device in those desolate surroundings.

Reaching down, she grasped a leather neck strap and pulled a camera from the burlap swaddle encasing it. She recognized it right away, having held it for Bobby a number of times as he climbed to a precarious vantage point to put more snapshots on his data card.

Ignoring the blink of the red battery light, she powered up the playback mode and cycled through the last dozen images. She braced herself for gruesome acts Bobby's probing lens might have captured on the farm, resolving not to faint or panic whatever she saw.

The shots of the property in late afternoon were eerie, but not explicitly horrific. Bobby could have presented them as an impressively photographed but gimmicky portrait of modern American Gothic. The landscapes would have lured a caravan of location scouts for the latest popular string of artsy, budget-conscious horror flicks. One image of the barn, backlit by late afternoon sun, disturbed her the most. It looked like a sealed, silent place for keeping the very worst of secrets. Katy couldn't account for the evil feeling that picture gave her, but she believed in it as keenly as any fact she could prove.

Something in one of the final images distracted her from the scuffle of approaching feet, until their owner was nearly upon her. A sturdy-looking farm truck was just visible in a low-angle shot of the farmhouse. She couldn't determine the details of its condition, but the windshield appeared intact and the hood was closed. Whether or not it proved to be a viable means of escape, it was worth checking out. She hoped it still sat in the farmyard, parked as close to the house as in the picture.

A thin whine of distress, far too close, disrupted Katy's internal flood of questions. The farmer's wife advanced from the darkness beyond the digital glow, the knife mowing the void before her like a tiny scythe. Katy barely dodged in time to save her chin. Remembering an old trick of Jimmy Stewart's from *Rear Window*, she thumbed the shutter button hoping to incapacitate her attacker with a flash. However, even an amateur like Bobby had enough artistic self-possession not to leave the device on its auto-flash setting. The camera clicked impotently, capturing what could have been a world-class nightmare image, before the enfeebled battery gave up and the camera winked out for good.

As the woman lined up another slash of the knife, her glance fell on the disturbed earth of the little nursery-graveyard. Katy received the biggest shock she could recall since before JT had opted to shoot a stranger's dog dead. The farmer's wife broke her customary whimper and spoke a few words in a whisper so sad, lucid, and soft that the smothered humanity of who and what she'd once been spoke directly to Katy across the time of her degeneration.

"I tried for 'em," said the farmer's wife. "Every gone sprout of 'em."

Katy heard the words clearly, and her heart could grind itself raw on their significance later. Survival reflexes moved her arm into action against every trace of her surprised empathy. She swung the camera sidelong by the strap, without a thought for the weeping puncture wound on her aching shoulder.

The camera connected with the old woman's face, unseating the bridge of her nose, caving in one cheek with a wet snap of cartilage and brittle jaw. The farmer's wife went down like a dropped rag. Sailing from Katy's grip, the camera broke into fragments when it struck the farmhouse wall.

Given time, Katy might have searched for the tiny digital card holding the chronicle of their journey. In a future so remote that she could scarcely picture any details of it, JT might want such a record. Then again, he might prefer to wipe the card or stomp it into shards unviewed. The urgency of getting back to him with the tatters of new information she'd gathered, and the frail hope of a workable plan, made it impossible to stay longer and look.

Katy suppressed an urge to apologize to the prostrate woman at her feet. She no longer had it in her to feel sorry for others just then. Beneath crisscrossed planks all bristly with nail heads, a window teased escape to the yard outside, but a shattered camera was no tool for prying or chopping her way out. Besides, she did not know what lay outside that window, and if JT hadn't been carried past the point of rescue, his predicament needed immediate attention.

She jerked like a fish at the sight of something slouched against the wall nearest the door. At first, she took it for a knot of scarecrows ready to spring. Stooping to grab a large chunk of camera lens that lay close to hand, she pitched it overhand into the shape and heard only a soft rustle of fabric. Nothing stirred.

Approaching, she could see that it was nothing more than a pile of old overalls, denim work shirts, flannels, jeans, plus a pair of canvas hip waders. A torn straw hat lay atop the heap, and Katy realized it was a kind of darning pile—discarded, recycled clothing obtained who knew when and where over the years. The farmer's wife could not have any proper washing methods available, but the thought of mending old garments to clothe new monsters—newly created scarecrows—lent a surprising dimension of warped domesticity to the disordered fog of her existence.

Katy grabbed a shirt which had pieces of wood and bone sewn on as replacement buttons. The top button appeared to be a once-healthy human molar. Katy had always been squeamish about tooth pain, and it froze her blood to imagine stolen teeth being put to any household use. Despite the prevailing rottenness of the home they kept, these farm folks wasted little.

The clothes were stiff and stained, no doubt infested with chinch bugs or worse. Katy recalled a conversation with Lisa long ago in which two words—"camouflage" and "mimicry"—flickered like an EXIT sign above a fire door. She knew their visit to the farm was approaching a final crisis. She would have to play her next moves with care, and a lot of luck, if she meant to give herself and JT a chance of surviving the night.

CHAPTER TWO

It Makes No Difference

Reflecting semi-conscious on the last twelve to twenty hours, JT concluded that what he and his loved ones had driven headlong into was just another death pit kept by some cosmic avatar of Kenny Chase, the little sadist boy he'd wanted to eradicate from existence and very nearly had. The pit wore the disguise of a real place, possibly of a whole drought-ravaged county, but the absence of anything except cruelty and suffering gave it away. On the farm, forces beyond anything allowed by nature's laws held sway. At some long-gone starting point there might have been a recognizable order, some divine reason behind the flocks of mutant crows fighting back the half-human monsters made there. Hell, flip the telescope and maybe the farm itself was a weary god's design to harvest the world of its remaining humanity. The world was plenty undeserving of what good was left in it. In that case, the crows might be a devil's prank to delay the inevitable.

Either way, the distinction was lost. Over a prolonged stalemate, the farm had grown into a meaningless malignancy. Its only definite function was drawing in as much life as possible, to corrupt and consume in fruitless, ever-degrading cycles. The whole setup would have been little Kenny's ultimate wet dream – hell on earth, homegrown.

That made JT's mind up for him. He resolved with brutal clarity that no level of pressure could compel him to choose a side, as long as he stayed alive. Especially when the sides meant nothing. To hell with talk of false messiahs, and with questions of good or evil in the further extermination of this or that form of life. He and Katy were all that mattered. They needed to get clear of the conflict while the two sides were busy tearing at each other. Let the diseased world look out for itself.

As his reason thundered with brave declarations, his

muscles threatened to give out. He was losing the energy to thrash away from the farmer's dribbling outflow. His tense lips loosened and the farmer poked a bony finger between them, drawing blood as it scratched and twisted. Soon, if JT did not open, the probing digit would bore a hole through his cheek instead. Or if the farmer summoned a couple of straw ghouls to hold him, a piece of wood or an iron chisel would pry his jaws apart quickly enough. They only needed him to swallow a few mouthfuls of that horrible stuff, to take nourishment from the farm's wicked soil.

The image of the pulsing thing in the well danced before him again. The farm's orifice held the source. The burning in his eye, not quite potent enough to brainwash him, continued giving him fitful flashes of what could happen to him while he remained in its power, or what he could become if he embraced that power.

A ragged shape staggered in from the bowels of the farmhouse, where the farmer's weevil-headed witch had vanished in pursuit of Katy a short while ago. Now the farmer had summoned another helping hand. Scalding tears of dread parted the black muck around JT's eyes. Even enraged and ready to fight, he could not face the possibilities of the next few minutes without fear.

The farmer half-turned his face to the newcomer, his grip on JT unbroken. The scarecrow was slighter of build, less brawny than some of the others. Nausea twisted JT's guts with a horrible thought: *No no no, please not Lisa.*

He cocked an eye floorward with a painful twist of his head, expecting to see one of her telltale sneakers. Both feet were bare, but they retained the healthy color of living flesh. The scarecrow moved quickly, hefting a rusty-headed crack hammer in its gloved hand.

Not Lisa, JT was oddly certain…

He gritted his teeth, straining against the wires that held

him down. The hammer's head filled his vision, raised for a moment before the scarecrow brought it down.

The heavy tool struck the chair just behind the base of JT's neck. The wood separated and clattered in all directions. JT rolled with a *whuff* onto where his tailbone met spine, the side of his head smacking the ground close enough to bite the scarecrow's ankle. As he sucked wind back into his chest, a wild thought materialized.

Hot damn, I know those feet!

Katy had made a hell of a disguise for herself on short notice. JT did not like to imagine where those old clothes had been, how they must smell or what vermin had been lodging inside. The ruse had worked well enough to paralyze him with momentary certainty that his number was up. More importantly, it had misdirected the farmer, allowing her to get close.

As the hammer cocked for another shot, the farmer snorted like a whitetail buck sensing crosshairs over its heart. Understanding came too late, as Katy put both shoulders into an upsweeping sidelong stroke. She hit the farmer on his jaw, spinning his head hard to the right. The blow caused the traveler's controlling presence to recede or wink out briefly, revealing the farmer for the sad, used-up old fool he was for less than a second, before the sinister shadow renewed itself.

JT might have given up his last remnant of hope, if not for Katy's reappearance to bring his courage back. She swept the bug-eaten straw hat from her head and flashed him a look so flinty-keen that he flinched. Then she hauled him to his feet with a power that made his heart skip with loving admiration. She was all dynamite and determination.

The path was clear for flight, but JT shocked himself by betraying his own vow to cut and run, for Katy's sake, at the first whiff of opportunity. Before he knew what had happened, he was on the farmer, knees compressing the man's old empty guts and airless chest. His hands, heedless of the wire that still bound splintered hunks of wood to each wrist, squeezed the farmer's emaciated throat as the sallow gasping face went purple-black. JT muttered vile curses he neither heard nor understood—for Bobby, for Lisa, for himself and Katy. For a world that made Kenny Chase, he gave every ounce of might to choking away the farmer's final breath.

The busted old man seemed eager to give up his anguish, yet something forbade him to die. JT, despite his fatigue, should have had plenty of strength left to throttle a weak opponent. The traveler's influence held his efforts at bay. As JT strained to finish the job anyway, Katy threw an elbow around his neck and pulled him back.

"Grieve for them later," he thought she said. "Not here. It's no good here."

She was right. They got going.

They had not quite reached the farmhouse door when sound bloomed from the farmer's throat, massively loud. It was an alarm, no question, putting JT in mind of the old town siren he had heard a half dozen times in boyhood for fire, flood, and tornados. The ramshackle house walls vibrated, catching and amplifying the roar.

Crows poured from their hiding places among the corn, twirling in angry airborne swarms like hornets, ready for the fresh cataclysm of a new day. Across the yard, shabby battalions of scarecrows emerged from the barn with the obedient swiftness of early-rising farm hands, ready for work.

CHAPTER THREE

I Feel the Earth Move

The truck, on which Katy had hooked a fingernail of hope, sat less than thirty yards from the farmhouse doorway. To be precise, it sat on an uneven plinth of jagged bricks and cinder blocks. Its one remaining tire was more than halfway shredded off the rust-caked rim. The slashes were straight and even, suggesting that the farmer or his wife had repurposed the rubber from the vehicle. Whether they'd used it for homemade shoes, to flavor their poisonous cornstalk chowder, or for more obscure purposes was anyone's guess. The truck was a shrine to the patron saint of dead ends and fucked prospects. Or perhaps it was a monument in reverse, giving chance visitors a future glimpse of what lonely months and years of slow cannibalization could do.

She half expected JT to bitch at her for having brought him to a useless landmark while still well within reach of danger, but he was too many steps behind her train of thought even to understand why she was disappointed. And after all, she had gotten him out of that chair and out of the farmhouse. She'd also dropped Ma and Pa Kettle in their homicidal tracks, which seemed to have thrown the general scene into major confusion.

To Katy, the farm looked like a gargantuan anthill that some gigantic shoe had kicked over. The scarecrows prowled in disorderly circles, their waving arms ready to seize anything that was not their kind. The traveler's alarm call had brought them but not given them any definite marching order. Completing the chaos were the crows, thick as gnats in their airborne tornado formations. Meanwhile, the flightless ones crawled from among the rows to assault the scarecrows' booted legs, hamstringing with razor beaks and tearing the corn-and-human innards from those that lost their footing.

JT, pawing at his dirty eye, shouted above the commotion. "What... What the hell now?"

Katy took the question to mean what did she plan to do with the dead truck now that they'd reached it. "Never mind this," she said. She was watching the melee, the way the crows dove in strafing patterns, how the scarecrows lashed out in self-defense. She bobbed her head absently, counting and mapping.

"Katy!"

"Hold on to me." She thrust a shaking hand under his face. "It's not that far."

"Far to what?"

"The camper. We get inside, make sure nothing's waiting in there for us, then grab the jack or Bobby's bat, whichever we find first. Your dad's old fly rod, if we get desperate."

"Wait, back up! Run to the camper? It's gotta be two hundred yards, if you're feeling optimistic, and I'm not."

"Where else, then?"

"Katy, I've never run a touchdown in my life. Now we're running double that, through all of... this? We'll be hamburger."

"Don't let them tackle you," she said, and grabbed his hand, causing them both to wince as she compressed various wounds. "Ignore the crows. They're not what you should worry about. Just dodge those other...things and I think it'll be fine."

JT nodded. "Sure. Fine." His incredulous face told her that he had lost all sense of what the word "fine" might mean for the present. No doubt he was thinking of the crow that had attacked his ear – the farm's first taste of any of them. Now things had changed, and she needed him to trust that. A sprint through the chaos would reveal plenty.

He locked eyes with her. "All right." She felt his confidence and faith in the familiar squeeze of his hand. She didn't need to say "Go." They started running as one mind, one body.

Four crows got the drop on them, landing on their clasped hands and forearms to claw and bite. JT yanked his hand back, roaring wounded profanities. After shaking his arm free of their grasping talons, he saw that Katy had made it through the ambush. Darting between interlocked ghouls and their avian foes, she never broke course for the camper, which was barely visible under the squadron of black birds perched atop its roof.

"Katy!" JT shouted as his winged aggressors drove him back toward the house. "Katy!"

Whether they meant to separate husband from wife, or simply to keep JT behind for something, the birds hovered over Katy without interfering. Only JT's attempt to follow had met with hostile backlash.

The next crow that landed on his shoulder went for his eye. Its poking beak did not blind him, but a blur and a sting of pain clouded his eyesight. JT swatted the bird away, stumbling back on his heels until a chunk of brick tripped him. He thrust both elbows behind him to spare his backbone the worst of the fall. A dangerous twinge of pain shot up the left triceps into his armpit and shoulder. He needed refuge as long as these crows meant to continue bullyragging him. The pickup cab was both closer and more desirable than the half-destroyed chicken house.

Katy, meanwhile, might still have been running. JT had no idea whether she'd seen him fall behind. He crab-walked on his hands and heels back to the truck, staying low. Something sharp cut his palm, but he didn't pause to inspect it.

Resting his sore elbow against the passenger-side running board, he reached up for a hard tug on the door handle.

Whatever resistance he'd expected proved baseless. Time and wear had so obliterated the latch mechanism that the door swung open faster than he could lean away. Its edge caught him between the eyes, enough to hurt like a son of a bitch, and the handle broke off in his grip – an extra "fuck you" to crown the moment. The group of crows had veered away toward other business. He guessed they'd had no other mission than to keep him from fleeing too far.

JT might have taken the opportunity to vent a futile fit of temper, had not his pecked eye distracted him by starting to burn like a brush fire. He blinked furiously to clean it with tears, but the traveler's ichor clung stubbornly. More blinking brought slow focus, as his bad eye and worse eye continued feeding him very different perspectives. He doubted that the human brain was built to tolerate what he saw for long.

His vision couldn't fully penetrate solid bodies in his path, but looking into them he could see their individual life forces more strongly now, as pulsing cores of light. While not as useful as electronic night vision, it would help him navigate the farm's dangers in search of his next goal. He touched his tender, throbbing forehead as blood oozed down the bridge of his nose, feeling too thick and feverishly hot.

A couple of items had fallen from the storage well of the door onto his chest, then onto the ground as he raised himself to one knee. The first was a road map of Nebraska which, by its age and powdery fragility, had probably been drawn up around the time the state was ratified. Throwing it aside, he saw it crumble practically to dust before it hit the dirt. The second object was a road flare, possibly of similar vintage but still capped. This he pocketed.

JT looked around for what he aimed to destroy. His new sight revealed it, a short distance away and a few dozen feet straight down.

He rummaged on the rear floorboards of the cab, then

through the sea of detritus in the bed. He came up with a spider bite and some jagged nicks on his fingers, but not what he wanted. A few feet of rubber hose would do in a pinch, or a small pump of any kind. The most useful items he found were a plastic vinegar jug with the top shorn off to provide a quart or less of storage, and a thin funnel with a spout maybe ten useful inches long.

Kneeling beside the truck, he fitted the funnel into the mouth of the fuel tank. Thinking he was prepared, he crammed his face into the funnel and drew his breath in hard, trying to create suction with his pursed lips against the top of the stem. All he got was a head and chest full of sour diesel fumes. He fell onto his back, gagging and choking. He wouldn't waste his health on a second attempt. He had no chance of success with the available equipment. The biggest risk, as he understood it, would not be acute poisoning but lung damage from vomiting once he'd ingested the stuff. Only the certainty that he'd soon be dead anyway, or worse, gave him the boldness to try another approach.

Once, long ago, he'd traveled as a roadie for a friend's thrash metal band, Lymphomaniac, on a mini-tour of coastal Louisiana. Outside a biker bar in Houma, thieves had drilled a hole in their van's tank while the group argued with house management about getting paid for the gig. After narrowly escaping a physical altercation over the money, they'd found themselves stranded in the parking lot with no alternative but to ask some of the bar's unfriendly regulars for help.

Placing the vinegar jug next to his head, JT procured a thick nail and a chunk of cinder block from the general mess nearby. Whether determination or corrosion played the bigger part, it took him only half a dozen smart knocks with his improvised hammer and awl to puncture the fuel tank. At the last instant, he was sure he'd seen a spark, although it might have been a hallucination. Possibly the fuel had degraded so much that a mere spark did nothing, meaning all his effort might be wasted. The ugly soup smelled as it should have but oozed from the tank with even less urgency than the blood from JT's injuries, dropping gummy clots as it came.

All the time that JT was engaged in his dicey business, no crows came by to bother him. Their swirling commotion filled the sky, their attacks keeping the scarecrows occupied and off his case. It wouldn't last, but for once he took the birds' angry noise as a sign that he might be doing something right.

Katy was in no state to judge whether her tunnel vision was a product of dehydration, terror and desperation, or a protective corridor formed by the crows along her path to the camper. She still didn't care for the birds or what they had represented on the Nebraska leg of her journey. Their only good point seemed to be that they were the scarecrows' enemies. Whatever the cause, the effect was a grotesque and curiously heart-lifting miracle worthy of the book of Exodus.

Gazing left then right, she perceived walls of slick black plumage. Every few feet, a gloved hand would thrust through and grab at her. A cluster of crows would turn their beaks on the intruding hand, ripping stitches from the glove and peeling rancid flesh off the fingers beneath, until the scarecrow withdrew its arm once more.

One scarecrow got both hands into the mix, grasped a flailing bird and tore it in ragged halves, the way someone might rip a telephone book for a party trick. Syrupy crow's blood painted Katy's cheek. She looked into the scarecrow's hideous face and saw that one eye socket still had a withered human eye in it.

Her stomach hitched with anxious hiccups at the thought of

being turned into one of those horrible things, with some remnant of her living human self looking out through a burlap hood. Bounding with renewed energy toward the camper door, she said to herself and to her enemies, "Not today. Not ever."

When it came down to survival versus extinction, Katy had impressed herself with the will to fight. She had not been so brave or sure-footed since childhood. Even before a positive outcome was anywhere near the horizon, she tingled with savage glee at how shocked JT must be to see her holding her own against monsters and killer birds, now smeared in fresh blood.

Katy leaped inside and slammed the camper door behind her, so hard that the frame buckled inward a fraction of an inch. The manufacturers had not counted on adrenaline levels like hers coming into play during any camping scenario. It probably hadn't been field tested for bear attacks either, let alone what Katy heard pounding and scrabbling for entry seconds later. The interior rocked as the scarecrows hammered the vehicle from all sides.

Using one hand to steady herself, she searched the interior. The baseball bat, still her first choice of weapon, rested under one of the lower bunks. She was almost positive that the farmer had taken JT's shotgun.

All she found in the footlocker, besides a terminally shaken-up beer can, was the plastic shopping bag containing Bobby's open pack of pop rockets. Without a clear thought as to why, she stuffed the little cache of incendiaries into the roomy waistband of the canvas work pants she wore, tucking the tail of the flannel shirt over them. If her experience so far had taught her anything, it was that you never knew what the situation might demand.

A spark seized her, connected to a life that seemed remote despite their having left it behind so recently—cell phones. Katy would have bet no signal would reach within a fifty-mile radius of the farm, but assuming they kept doing their damnedest to escape, a time would come when they could be charged and used to summon help. She hoped JT had left the key in the lockbox where they'd stored the phones, or was it a combination—

Her brain cut off all speculation as the world lurched. It felt as if the camper meant to retch her out again into the mayhem of the cornfield. Katy gasped air to steady her own turning stomach, using the bat as a cane to keep herself from falling over as the camper gave another violent jostle.

Katy had been poised to bust as many heads as she could when the door eventually collapsed inward or fell off its hinges. However, the scarecrows had put their drone-lobes together and thought about the inefficient siege plan. They'd now gathered on one side of the camper and were attempting to tip it.

If they succeeded, their chances of getting inside would only dwindle. That was her last coherent thought before the third or fourth big shove finally overbalanced the vehicle and Katy went tumbling headlong into the wall. She landed in a splayed heap, ears ringing, on top of the door which was now blocked by the ground.

They hadn't managed to kill her, but Katy was nicely sealed inside. She banished the idea, however attractive, that she could rest for a few minutes in relative safety. The side camper window was now a skylight, and she'd better look for the easiest way to climb up and open it. Pushing herself up on her forearms, she groaned at a dull, radiating pain along her left side. Her torso had hit the built-in card table on her way down.

Another jolt came, along with a crash of glass. Katy rolled aside, just barely, to avoid being impaled by what looked like a small tree shoved through the camper's windshield. No, not a tree, but a stout wooden pole topped with a short crossbeam. A writhing figure in tattered farm duds much like her own clung to it. The scarecrows had shoved in a life-sized crucifix, complete with a volunteer from their ranks to ride its way in. Katy almost had to admire the savage ingenuity of the maneuver, but her focus was on the new exit hole the creatures had made for her.

The scarecrow squirmed off the pole and reared up before her, its hands snapping at her as if looking for the right place to grab a snake. Katy, who had sturdy footing, stepped into her swing with the bat.

The first blow fell in the hollow of the scarecrow's neck. The flesh made a campfire crackle as the sack-hooded head flopped down against its shoulder. They were brittle, yes, but some kind of skeleton persisted beneath all the rot. Unable to raise its head up straight again, the creature pawed at her undaunted.

She swung from overhead in a log-splitting motion, and smashed whatever thin membrane passed for a skull. Dark lumpy matter coughed out the bottom of the sack, and the figure sank to the floor like a malfunctioning Halloween prop. The limbs convulsed, but it did not rise again.

Katy's body tingled with a triumphant surge that soothed her pain for a few seconds. Then a new scarecrow scrambled through the windshield frame and crawled down the pole like a lizard into the cabin.

"Stop this, God damn you!" Katy bellowed.

Evidently, word had not spread among the scarecrow hordes about her ability to wield a Slugger. She swung so hard against the second monster's pelvis that the wood splintered with a grand-slam crack. Left holding an ash wood stake, she stabbed holes in its body and head with a glee that under normal circumstances would have been unsettling.

She moved backward from the cab, watching the windshield for any more trouble. Her bare toe stubbed against the broken table, reminding her that she was barefoot, and that she knew a lot of filthy words that she saved for special occasions.

Her toe throbbed as she searched the upset cabin, the nailbed bulging black with a painful hematoma. Pulling herself up, biceps screaming, she balanced her heel on a fire extinguisher box and opened the locker beside her bunk. Her trail runners fell out, along with an open toiletries bag. Katy's grip slipped and she nearly followed them down, where she might have bent her spine backwards over the edge of the opposite bunk. She caught herself with a trembling arm, and lowered herself to a safe position where she could grab the shoes.

Lacing up, feeling the insoles hug her arches, she drew a clearer lungful of air than she had for days. Her gaze focused on the vehicle's rear wall, where the push-out emergency window awaited her. She didn't care to mess with a third kamikaze scarecrow in the close cabin quarters if she could help it.

Moving across the cabin toward the back, she found the tire jack wedged under a bunk strut. She had to work the whole assembly loose before she could slide the handle free. After disengaging the safety catches on the exit window's lower corners, she used the jack handle to push it outward, listening for movement and holding her body as far back from the opening as possible.

A crow clawed its way up onto the sill, startling a yelp out of her. It looked Katy up and down, preened behind its wing, then favored her with three hostile caws.

Focusing her hatred on the black fluttering silhouette, she lifted and heaved the jack barrel. "Squawk now, loudmouth," she said as the jack made the bird and the window disappear with a crash.

Katy was moving in the next instant, vaulting through the dislodged frame and out among the rows. The end of her

Slugger-spear dripped black ichor and stank of corn liquor.

The comfort of her own shoes, after hours barefoot on that hellish terrain, gave Katy a quick shock of pleasure. Had she been forced out of the camper before finding them, she might have ended up with two soles full of window glass.

The first scarecrow lunged around from the side of the camper, arms thrown out before it. Katy thrust the jagged bat into its middle, just under where she judged the ribs to sit. The scarecrow twisted, pulling the bat handle from her hand. Grabbing it again, she pulled the creature in close before hammering its head to corn pudding with the steel jack rod.

A scarecrow jumped from atop the camper and seized her by the shoulders from behind. Dropping her body into its wiry grip, she lifted both feet off the ground to kick the Slugger deeper into the scarecrow in front of her. With a crack of spinal column, it snapped at a right angle.

Reaching back to search for weak spots as the second scarecrow tried wrestling her to the ground, she felt a jagged tusk of rib. Grasping it, she wrenched downward as if to release a stuck parking brake. The rib snapped off close to the sternum. Tossing it away, she reached into the opening she'd made and touched a hot, wet mass deep inside the scarecrow's torso. The feeling of it between her fingers pushed a sick belch up her throat, but she gripped and yanked it loose for good measure. The scarecrow juddered like a stalling car, its arms releasing Katy as it fell sideways to the earth.

She collapsed half a dozen burlap-covered skulls with two-handed swings of her jack handle, and swept almost as many pairs of legs at the knees, relishing the opportunity to paste a few more of the ugly fuckers.

Four more appeared from the dark, hoisting another of the toppled cross-poles they'd used on the camper windshield. Before Katy could make an evasive move, they rammed her down with a rough thump of timber against her hip. Tumbling into a headlong sprawl, she opened both hands to protect her face from hitting the ground. The jack handle went flying into the dark. She heard the muted crash of its landing in the dense vegetation.

A dozen scarecrows closed on her, hoisting her aloft as she thrashed and cursed them. A moan rose from her throat at the loss of both her skull-busting weapons, and her neck craned for the best possible view.

The darkness had a curious glow to it, as if dawn wanted to break, but some wicked force held it at bay for just a little longer than normal. Once converged on a single objective, the scarecrows acted as orderly as a swarm of bees. They turned one by one from the camper to follow the captive's procession through the rows and across the yard. In seconds only a few were left around the camper, dealing moronic parting kicks to the roof before the hive-signal caught them and they turned on their heels for home.

A massive black wooden edifice rose in Katy's view, the one she had hated at first sight. Its innards belched smoke and creosote. A pair of straw-clad acolytes opened the portal to a yawning maw.

They were going to the barn.

CHAPTER FOUR

To Live is To Fly

JT was thankful that he had more to guide him than his natural sight as he staggered along the fringe of the farmyard mayhem. Night seemed to flake away as dawn loomed indefinitely. A profusion of black flecks whirled and dove, cawing desperately, to peck at the mob of confounded and turned-about scarecrows. The scene, although their escape set it in motion, had taken on a profound momentum of its own.

The birds and the scarecrows were fighting as if they meant this to be the final battle, with the possibility of total mutual eradication. All attention seemed to be off JT, though he did not expect that indifference to last.

He followed the painful visions in his damaged eye as though in a trance. In truth, it was more of a bad drug trip—wheezing from the traces of broken-down diesel he'd aspirated and unavoidably swallowed. What a stupid idea that had been. He prayed, if his disordered thoughts could be called prayer, that any poisoning would be acute and short-lived. The vision in his intact eye—the improving one—fuzzed and flexed in a psychedelic lantern show that no willing person would pay to see.

The bad eye, now…that was where things got interesting.

Facing the corn, he beheld acres of luminescent stalks waving like kelp in the glowing seabed that was the soil. The life force powering the farm's hideous outgrowth, and animating its unholy keepers, came from the groundwater.

Looking more carefully, he perceived clusters of long veiny roots, despite their being many feet underground. These extended from the fields through the earth beneath the house, terminating somewhere beyond the barn. They appeared to irrigate the land constantly, or perhaps impregnate it from the way they strained and pulsated with lewd effort.

Sliding along the side of the barn, JT felt the proximity of his goal as a low-voltage buzz in his brain. He hadn't been certain from the various impressions, hallucinations and intuitions flooding his thoughts whether or not the well was open or filled in. If he would have to dig or drill to reach whatever he was meant to find, he might as well give up the search and let himself be drawn, quartered and relegated to the corn-demon life.

He drew near the weed-shrouded well cap, a round pallet of desiccated, rot-curled planks nearly flush with the ground. The wood was so powdery with decay that JT had little trouble kicking it in. He nearly lost his footing as bits of the concrete lip crumbled underfoot. In that suspended moment, sunrise seemed an uncertain bet, but the sky had brightened enough to confirm what he had seen before in his mind's eye.

The thing in the well, sunk no more than a dozen to fifteen feet, clung to the rubble walls like a web of fungus. Delicate shoots like bird's nesting twigs anchored it in place, while at the center a knobbed protrusion, like a grotesque mushroom, jutted above the larger mass. It was curiously familiar to JT, because he'd seen traces of it in the fluid presence occupying the dark crevices of the old farmer. Sensing the energy that surged from it, he had no doubt that whatever personality lay at the center of that inert tumor clogging the well, it had carved its own shadow loose to possess the farmer and wear his flesh. This, he thought as he stared down past his toes, this was the entity—mammary, ovary, seminal vessel—sustaining the corn and all it represented.

A number of arcane and sanctified methods might have existed to sterilize it, castrate it, abort it, but JT was no shaman. At best he was a strain of semi-reformed Gulf Coast hippie, too cynical for mystic thinking. He might have been shy on spiritual intuition, but he doubted whatever cosmic cowpie had birthed all this unpleasantness would be vulnerable to anything as tidy as a magical incantation. As America's corn crib geared up for a premature apocalypse, perhaps the solution could be as simple as good old-fashioned combustion. He tossed his jug of flecked, syrupy diesel into the hole, giving the container a spin to coat the matter below as evenly as possible. JT had never met a man, beast, fowl, or germ that responded pleasantly to fire.

Katy suppressed a retch at the fetid atmosphere in the barn loft. She chose playing possum as her best tactic, giving her captors no more help than a bale of hay, until she understood her surroundings better. As they stuffed her up the ladder and through the hatchway, she thrust her right hand sideways to grasp a length of rust-pitted chain dangling over the frame. It might have been used to pull or fasten a hatch door in bygone days. The scarecrows shoved against the unexpected resistance. The links bit a rusty crease into her palm before one of them gave way. Seven or eight inches of chain came off in her fist. Before her captors could notice and confiscate it, she curled her hand into her sleeve cuff and dropped it down inside the shirt fabric to rest near her elbow.

Everywhere she looked, scarecrows guarded the entrances, exits, hidey-holes and other likely places for her to scamper. However the farm worked its evil will, she was trapped in its dirty core. The farmhouse ordeal had taught her an interesting lesson: by plotting her escape from all the way inside, she could better avoid any dead ends or surprises that might await her if she cut and ran blindly. It just might take that much more time and effort to claw her way out again.

The stench here was so potent that she realized she'd been smelling it faintly almost the whole time they'd been on the farm. Mulchy hay odor and sweet manure funk were mere undertones. The smell had a property of decay overreaching any biological musk, from compost to slaughterhouses, that she could imagine. The entire building exhaled its own rancid corpse breath, interlaced with the moonshine sharpness of half-rotten corn in some abominable eternal stew.

As they set her down roughly on the sagging planks of the loft, a rank hot breeze washed across her skin—not a cleansing kitchen steam, but a vapor that left deposits in the pores and tickled the eyes unpleasantly. It came from a huge cauldron, something a fairy-tale witch might possess for cooking children in. She was uncomfortably close to the coals that kept it simmering. A scarecrow that must once have been a very large person towered over her, stirring the concoction with a sludge-caked hoe handle.

Katy's right arm was stretched out stiff to the side. Her fingers picked idly at the boards, finding them gritty and pasty. She realized with queasy shock that she'd pushed dried blood deep under her nails. Someone else's blood, possibly even Bobby's or Lisa's. The area where she'd been set was ringed with old gore, the sacrificial circle of some dark religion. She had no interest in converting.

A work boot pressed down with slow, unapologetic force on her left wrist. It hurt like hell, but she kept her fist closed. Another scarecrow put its foot on her right wrist, and Katy held her position despite the agony of two almost-solid humanoid forms bearing down on her arms.

She almost cried out at the sight of what hung in the rafters, holding vigil over the stinking corn-fueled rite. Three withered, naked, black-green ghouls unrecognizable as once having been live humans, dangled from chain and hook tackle. Torn sagging flesh hung from them in pendulous pouches. One had a single wisp of long white hair clinging to its scalp. The jawbones were agape, a result of dried corncobs jammed partway into their gullets. One figure had its throat cut, the gash revealing dark resinous matter that clogged the bulging esophagus. Their abdomens were all grossly distended.

Katy had an intuition, impossible to prove, that the arrangement of the bodies made an almost readable diagram of the process. Those people had been stuffed with the vile home-brewed corn porridge to the top of their throats, no doubt gagging in their death throes as their obsolete organs were pulled out their navels to make more space from beneath. Possibly the old cobs had been used as rams to ensure total saturation. Whether they were instructional models or trophies of the work carried out there, the corpses illustrated what would most likely befall anyone brought inside the barn.

Katy pondered these hanging atrocities, and what they meant for her immediate future, with a kind of unquestioning numbness. Her strongest feeling in the moment was a conviction that she would leave the barn as herself, alive or dead. She would find a way to keep from becoming suitable material for a scarecrow. She'd passed on the chance to succeed the farmer's wife, and she was not about to take a demoted role in the same organization.

A puff of hot sparks from under the cauldron singed her face. The momentary smell of her own burning hair was practically a relief, and it brought her back in step with reality. Despite her thirst and her many pains, Katy hadn't spent the last of her energy.

When she saw the hooked blade one of the scarecrows brandished as it approached her—some kind of rusted skinning tool, second cousin to a linoleum knife—she nearly let her bladder go. Biding one's time was fine, but had she only been stalling inevitable horrors too long? She had to choose the perfect time to throw up a diversion. There always was one—in sports, in professional struggles, in social tangles. What made Nebraska zombie rituals any different?

She felt the first slash open her up, a traditional autopsy incision from collarbone to pelvis. The sear of pain was so real that she yelped before realizing that her terrified imagination had supplied the sensation. The first cut had merely been to open the flannel shirt down the front. Aside from a short slit in her own shirt underneath and a tiny nick above her belly button, the gesture had an almost surgical deftness. Her tooth-and-bone buttons clattered away over the boards.

The hefty scarecrow lifted its stirring stick out of the pot, letting hot slime fall off in clumps. It was either checking the consistency or letting Katy see what to expect next, in case she had not figured it out.

With Katy pinned by her now-purple wrists, there was no way to work the shirt off her arms without letting her up. To solve this, the scarecrow slit a neat seam down the length of the left sleeve. Katy clenched her fist tighter and counted silently to steady herself as the blade started up the right sleeve.

The cutting tool gouged the sensitive inside of her elbow, but the pain was minimal. When the blade struck the chain links loosely encircling her forearm, one of them snagged the point and dragged against the floorboards with a harsh clatter. It was disruption enough, but barely.

The scarecrow with its foot on her shied back, the tiniest aversion to sudden stimulus. Katy drew her arm up her sleeve and inside the loose shirt, like a racer snake escaping into a burrow. The motion toppled the scarecrow and sent its buddies into consternation. Her left hand was almost asleep and useless, but she forced it to reach inside the trouser waistband to retrieve Bobby's grab bag of partly smashed but otherwise dry and viable fireworks. Her shorts under the scarecrow pants still held JT's lighter, which she had confiscated during their foreplay.

A scarecrow rushed forward and tried to stomp on her chest. She whipped her chain in a viper strike at its ankle, then caught its hovering boot and shoved. The scarecrow toppled backwards into a sagging joist.

Three more of them advanced on her, and she was not yet on her feet. She scarcely had time to light the fuses on a small sheaf of Roman candles before they were within grappling distance. Kicking out at the leader's pelvis, she threw the lit wands where it had been standing. The Roman candles landed between the other two creatures, which turned to watch as brilliant fluorescent fireballs belched forth in all directions.

The barn caught fire, aided by haphazard piles of corn husks, dry straw, and scraps of fabric. The scarecrows ran to stomp and smother individual pockets of flame. Even they had to fear something. A few made headway against the blaze, but many more caught fire. It was quite a thing to see those reanimated horrors panic, unable to cry for help beyond thin hisses.

"How about a little fire, scarecrows?" The words were out before she was conscious of forming them.

The loft filled with smoke much more quickly than she'd anticipated. She flung a firecracker string, the sound making her ears clang. Then she lit two twelve-packs of skyrockets without unwrapping the cellophane sleeve that bound them together. She'd seen Bobby toss these improvised grenades at JT's feet while he was busy grilling steaks or pumping up an inner tube, with predictable hilarity. Flinging them as far into opposite corners as she could, she pushed her sore body up to a running stance. Cookfire smoke made her eyes burn and run.

The big scarecrow swung its wooden staff at her. She screamed as a scalding glob of chunky tar struck her cheek and neck. Smoke rushed into her airway, turning her cries into coughs.

Fuck it. Unmindful of the blistering heat, she grabbed the flailing end of the stirring pole and pitched her full body weight back against it. Tumbling onto her butt, she scooted away fast as the overstuffed monster splashed into the bubbling pot. She rolled to avoid the steaming eruption of corn-mess across the rapidly burning timbers.

The oxygen level in the barn had significantly diminished, and Katy's adrenaline wasn't much better. She tried to take a step but her knee buckled. Flaming scarecrows rolled and charged in every direction, but so many had crowded the ladder hatch that the way was sealed off for Katy. Climbing the rafters to search for a gap in the roof would be a dicey prospect even at her peak strength. Now it amounted to suicide.

The lone ray of daylight threw a mottled pool on the floor. The window for letting sun in, and possibly for shoving hay bales through on any normal farm, was wired over with rusty poultry mesh. Slivers of glass and bent metal decorated the gridwork, woven into it at random. Several black feathers clung to the barrier, held on by clots of blood and ruffled by breezes.

Aiming for the outer edges so as not to kick through the middle and deli-slice her ankle, Katy pummeled the covering with both feet. The staples began to give after the third blow, encouraging her to wind up for a strong finish. The impact of her supine mule-kick freed both sides and tore out the lower trim board fastened to the bottom. The screen flapped outward, revealing a jagged sill left by the separated wood.

With no time to be choosy about her exit options, Katy rolled to her stomach and crawled toward the window hole. Tiny splinters bit her palms. The edge of the loose-hanging mesh clawed tracks in her arms and the back of her neck. In the dark she saw a slapdash heap of bales, probably old and pest-eaten, twenty feet below. She rotated her body to crawl out feet first, and lowered herself with a vicious burn of lactic acid in her shoulders.

The hay did not break her fall, but it saved her shins and

tailbone from snapping. She wobbled to her knees like a newborn foal, catching a thin whistle of breath before she could walk. The lack of light had prevented her from seeing a hay fork half-buried under the moldering straw. Her body had missed its wicked tines by the scant width of her last remaining hope.

She heard scrabbling feet across bare earth inside the barn. Scarecrows were coming, probably on fire and certainly not worried about what they trampled in their flight. Katy stooped and grabbed the old fork. She knocked the rust off a large hasp which swung to fit over a catch on the doors, then fitted the tool's handle through it.

Witch in the oven, Gretel.

The improvised bolt would not hold the scarecrows long, but it might be enough to burn them down to a more manageable number. Katy leaned on her knees, ambushed by a heavy coughing fit.

Morning had broken. In fact, the way things looked, it might have been permanently shattered.

The whistle and bang of rockets in flight, muffled but unmistakable from where he stood behind the barn, turned JT around in a hurry. He'd just pulled the flare from his pocket, set it down on the damp earth next to the well rim, and removed the ignition cap to examine it. The sound of rapid footsteps around the side of the building would have put him in a fighting stance, if not for the distraction of nostalgic sounds from the loft above.

A second later the fireworks were inside his brain as the farmer rounded the corner and swung the shotgun muzzle against the side of JT's head. The blow felt as if it spun his head all the way around, when in truth it only knocked him a quarter turn off his footing. That was enough to send one shoe skidding into the well. JT's body, already losing the battle with gravity, followed close behind.

He caught himself on the lip with a jolt of pain from his elbows up through his chest and shoulders. His trunk and legs dangled inside the well's astonishingly chilly throat. Digging elbow points and broken fingernails into the loamy dirt and catching the outer rim of the well's masonry, he found a precarious hanging point that might hold a few minutes if nothing disturbed his balance.

The farmer wrestled with the gun, trying to load it on his hip using the tremulous, arthritic claws that served him for hands. JT had nothing to compare to the picture of age, malnutrition, and disease before him, but the farmer's devastated condition went against everything he'd ever heard about the benefits of wholesome country life. The twisted old bastard looked barely strong enough to hold the gun shoulder height again.

At point blank range, it was easy enough for the farmer to rest the muzzle against JT's forehead. Watching the gnarled index finger creep into the trigger guard, JT shifted his weight to one arm and batted the barrel aside. The concussion of the blast, amplified by the well, made JT's head feel as though it were exploding. One of his ears went immediately deaf, which he hoped would be temporary but didn't have time to worry about. He had limited stamina for any further maneuvers, and the farmer was already struggling to rack the old pump-loader's action.

Searching with his hands for anything to help deflect, obstruct, or wound, he snapped a forked sliver off the largest piece of well cap, extending his reach by several inches. When the barrel of the Browning swiveled his way again, he jabbed the muzzle downward before the farmer could plant his feet for another shot. The muzzle sank into the dirt a good four or five inches, pushed in by the stumbling farmer's belly against the stock.

With a full-body spasm that hurt all the way down his legs, JT flopped himself the short extra distance he needed to grab the stuck gun. It provided a brace for him to pull a knee out of the well. The farmer was still bent over the gun, which he'd been trying to tug free, and he registered JT's reappearance on solid ground just before JT wrapped both hands around the barrel and yanked upward. The gun stock smashed the bridge of the farmer's nose. His facial tissue gave with a wet pop – bad news for either his lateral cartilage or the orbital bone under his eye socket, or both.

The farmer's nostrils bubbled with blood. He bared his teeth in a yellow sneer. JT wanted nothing more than to turn the gun around and put that dirty old dog down, but the gun wouldn't be safe to fire until he could bore all that impacted mud out. Almost every kid watched horrendous road crash videos in driver's ed classes, but JT and Bobby's dad had sent them through a Texas hunter's safety course as well. JT had seen the damage that muzzle blockages did to well-built firearms and their operators.

He appeased his rage by snatching the gun back and using it to club the farmer across the temple. The farmer sank to the ground with a wet, fishy gasp. JT would have stomped his brains out where he lay, but a distant scream from Katy stopped him. He had business to conclude.

The road flare poked from the soft earth where JT had left it before the fight started. He had dropped the cap with the striking edge, probably into the well, when the farmer hit him. His heart surged with panic until he noticed blood welling on his knuckles. He'd scraped them raw against the jagged, falling-away rim of the well.

Seizing the flare, he swiped the ignitor across the rough

concrete and turned his face away as a searing flame shot from its end. His eyes naturally fell downward, and the sight below made a permanent impression on his mind.

The flare threw a brilliant red crackle of light against the well's interior. The corresponding shadows jumped and danced. JT tried vainly to assure himself that the movement was only an effect of that illusion, but a deeper part of him insisted that the traveler's faceless head was twisting upward to regard him. A hollow opened to represent a mouth, and the thin shriek from it sounded like a corroded hinge on hell's door.

JT realized he was clutching the flare for dear life. He willed his fingers to drop it, hoping the thing had a good strong burn left in it. The belch of heat and light let him know that whatever lived in death down there had caught fire. Seconds later, a faint tremor under the ground signified the farm taking notice that its heart was burning to ash.

The farmer's foot rammed out, kicking JT hard in the ankle. JT toppled, snarling in pain and surprise, and the fall knocked some of the wind out of him. The farmer pushed up onto both knees and found his feet first.

A jagged stone, possibly part of a brick, struck the old man in the ear. It thudded in the dirt with blood on its edge. Katy came at a purposeful stride, her arm still extended from the throw, her face displaying a readiness to do damage.

The farmer surprised them both. He pivoted his torso to show that he'd picked up the gun, and swung it upward in Katy's direction. Knocked in and out of his eroded consciousness, he must have either forgotten or failed to register the weapon's inoperative condition. A catastrophic misfire might still propel a fatal plug of mud into Katy's chest, and that realization restored JT's breath. He bent his legs under him and frog-hopped from his position on the ground, choosing the shorter distance to his wife and tackling her at the knees just as the farmer pulled the trigger.

The combustion split the chamber, snapping it partway off the stock and blowing back most of its force over the farmer's shoulder. Shrapnel wiped away the farmer's cheek and a goodly chunk of his ear on that side, as if the flesh were makeup easily toweled off. He stood dazed, eyes furiously twitching as if to dislodge the bad fortune that had backfired on him. The raw tissues of his face glistened, red and wet with streaks of powder burn. He wobbled on his feet with braindead inertia.

None of his minions came to his aid. The scarecrows had lost all interest in their farmyard rumble and went running into the fields, where tongues of fire appeared to have sprung up from the cornstalk roots and now licked at the dearly sown bounty. Not spread from the source in the well, exactly, but transmitted through the shared soil. Whether the creatures had some aim of putting out the flames or were charging into a suicidal pact of self-immolation, JT did not much care. The creatures gradually lost control of their limbs, their drunken gait causing them to collide with one another as they continued into the rising cornfield fire. Half the crows gathered in an aggressive formation to herd stragglers along with the group. The rest of the birds hovered and circled, waited and watched.

The farmer's wife appeared, her knife out and ready to carve. JT hissed as the slashing blade opened a slit high in his quivering right shoulder, just below the base of his neck. Spinning to meet his attacker, he scarcely recognized her in the daylight. Half her face was bruised purple and swollen, as if someone had clocked her a bad one across the side of the head since he'd encountered her last.

"Knock it off," was the only retort he could muster, cupping the fresh wound and dodging backward against her renewed slashes. He wasn't sure of his bearings and reasoned dimly that she was backing him into the well again.

"Damn you," Katy growled, advancing. "We said cut that shit out!" She grabbed the old woman's wrist, letting her dance like a trapped moth, sweeping her blade in wild perilous arcs.

What stopped her violence was not the spite of the young interlopers but the arrival of a crow broken away from the rest. It fluttered down onto Katy's forearm, within easy pecking distance of the farmer's wife. Katy let it dig its cruel talons in, and shoved it toward the stricken face of the woman.

Take her eyes. JT surprised himself with the vengeful thought, and his wish for a grand finale for the night's brutal cycle of eye trauma. Fair was only fair.

Instead, the crow made a harsh caw of recognition. It was enough to send the farmer's wife into a screaming fit. She jerked her hand free of Katy's grasp, throwing the knife aside but managing to slit Katy's thumb webbing as she did. With a howl of terror, the madwoman of the farm sailed to the side of her husband. Turning to face her, he opened his mouth as if to mutter a soothing word or issue a soft command. What came out instead was more of his black bile-tar.

The traveler emptied all that remained of its tenacious essence, made up of more fluid than one man could naturally hold. The farmer vomited quarts of the stuff, slopping it in gouts over his wife's face as she continued to scream. The traveler sought a warmer body without hesitation. What did not stick to the woman ran down to form slick pools around their feet. Tendrils and pseudopods extended from it, testing the air like reptile tongues until they pointed in Katy's direction. The black mess, feeble but inexorable, came for her.

Backing Katy away, JT slipped in the advancing ooze and went to his knees. Katy muttered something profane yet uplifting and jerked him roughly up again. At the same moment, the farmer's half-alive form slumped to his knees, pulling his clinging wife down along with him. The dim eyes of the past gave an earnest look to the present. Any future was out of their hands. The farmer grasped his wife's hand and lifted his arms, as if welcoming the end.

The crows made no allowance for Katy and JT as they dove in a frenzied cyclone. The young couple pulled each other clear after the first round of talons and beaks grazed them. From a distance of a dozen yards, they watched, neither able to turn away as the birds tore and shredded the flesh of both farmer and his wife from their shuddering bones. The flightless mutants came crawling like rodents to consume the bubbling, still-struggling residue of the traveler. They peeled it off the bare ground in squishy wormlike gobbets and gulped it down. A crow with a brick-sized goiter in place of one leg even crept over to JT and picked spatters of the foul stuff off his leg. It did so with no particular gentleness, but JT let it finish.

For a long time, no words passed between Katy and JT. It seemed indecent to contaminate the air with professions of amazement, with questions, with grim jokes. It was a scene for witnessing, not for commenting upon. After such a long time of noise and chaos, the crows feasted in silence.

CHAPTER FIVE

Going Out West

By the time the sun was fully up, it would have been difficult to prove that a working farm had stood on the land within the past decade. The greenery had putrefied at the speed of time-lapse footage, and dried to dust in little more than an hour. The farm had rushed through its decay, as if penitently making up for its long spell of unnatural robustness. The last ears of what had masqueraded as prize corn were withered now to semi-liquid frailty. A handful of leaning stalks were sloughing them off like scabs.

Even the crows had lost interest in the crops, turning instead to pick the bones of scarecrow carcasses clean. The edible fragments of the nearly gone monstrosities were the closest thing to decent feed within reach. Their sudden docility in the farm's death throes, after the consumption of farmer and wife, had reassured Katy and JT that any immediate danger had passed. Even so, the birds continued their ghoulish devouring ritual until dawn peered from the east. They followed the bidding of something unseen but almost tangible in the rot-scented air, to do away with every possible trace.

The farmhouse and henhouse had burned to cinders. A single partial wall of the barn stood, though a stiff gust might blow it to dust and probably would. The elements would consume these remnants without trouble or delay, as readily as the scorched sea of corn stalks. Soil would sweep over the bones and clot the dead well shut before long. It seemed a thing ordained.

In the morning light, the farm was utterly leached of color, an antique photograph of bad times barely remembered. JT had gone to the camper, after hearing Katy tell of her narrow escape, without much hope of salvaging any useful supplies. Mainly, he had done it to kill time while she rested her battered body.

More than anything, he hadn't wanted to see the birds pull dead flesh off the scarecrows. He could not face the idea that somewhere nearby, his baby brother's remains were joining the fossil record. Lisa, too, unless she had burned to ash. There would be time to weep for them and drink to them, as Katy had said, but only if the survivors kept surviving.

Katy could not be ready to dwell on family tragedies either. Guessing the severity of her pain was as simple as looking at her. She winced with every breath. Ugly bruises up one side of her torso, from her hip to just under her left breast, told a vivid story.

Despite her account of the camper's destruction, JT had entertained a slim hope of salvaging something useful. He stared at the charred timber jutting from the windshield and understood how much worse it was than what he'd expected. The camper was a twisted, smoldering garbage heap. After the rough treatment it received from the scarecrows, burning corn stalks had collapsed through the broken side window that now faced up. The interior smelled nice and cooked. Their vehicle and any cargo of value belonged to time and the elements now. Perhaps a wanderer would discover it before it weathered and subsided beyond recognition, but anyone who might pass by would shun it if they were wise. It was no longer a shelter for the lost souls it had carried the previous day, a juggernaut bound for oblivion and doom.

JT's eye still hurt. The sliced upper lid reopened every few minutes, reminding him of the injury with a petulant sting. His vision on that side retained a sense of color, light, and some movement, but he feared that proper cleaning and dressing would only restore it partway. He wouldn't be likely to stake his life or future livelihood on marksmanship.

Not only pain but resignation, possibly a permanent rupture of his lifelong stubbornness, prompted him to leave the camper to its own destiny. An impression, clear but not quite substantial enough to call a voice, had come to him as he vainly thrust an arm between jagged spurs of wood, hoping to reach a screwdriver and a roll of tape from the broken-open emergency kit. He had vague notions of splinting one or another of Katy's injuries.

With the sudden clarity of cold water on the neck, JT had understood that nothing was to be taken away, not even what they had brought along with benign intentions. Not so much as a can of beer, toted hundreds of miles in a spirit of glad-hearted brotherhood, had escaped corruption. The man and woman were left only with their lives and what remained of the garments on their backs. If they could not thrive or be content with that, it was their problem.

He found her sitting up, an improvement from when he had left her, facing the large fence gap leading out to the main road. The empty view on both sides made it difficult to recall how thoroughly the ramparts of abnormal greenery had obscured their position from sight. Katy had turned her back on the farm and its crumbling vestiges, all of JT's recent epiphanies having evidently occurred to her already.

"Katy," he whispered.

She did not stir, stalling the future with a moment's prolonged meditation. Unless, he thought, she had decided to check out after all.

"Kate," he said with a weak snap of his fingers. "We okay?"

Katy took several long, slow, wincing breaths.

"No," she said. "Tomorrow morning, and the next… every morning we wake up from now on, we're going to think long and hard about whether we want to wake up again. We're dangerously dehydrated, miles from any way of fixing it. I doubt you'll get your sight back in that eye. I can… ahhh… still walk, but I'll be damned if I don't have a cracked rib. Your gun is broken. If we can find medical help before tetanus gets us, it will be a miracle.”

“Damn, darlin’.” JT hardly recognized the feeble sound of his own laugh. “That rosy outlook never lets you down.”

“Just wait, babe,” she said. “When the shock wears off, we’ll both feel a hell of a lot worse.”

“So,” JT said. The word was a declarative, not a question. He wished he could refute, or even bring himself to doubt, her gloomy assessment of how their chances stood. He stared westward for a minute or two. It had to be west because the sun, just over his back, had already begun warming his neck.

“So,” he ventured again, “let’s go?”

For ten seconds, he was cold with certainty that Katy had died. Then she gave a horrible hitching gasp, either reacting to or preventing a laugh.

“Yeah,” she wheezed. “We’ll go.”

They headed west. At some point, a distance JT no longer found himself able to dream, the horizon would turn green and rise up as mountains before them. There might be bears or angry moose, but no acres of corn.

Helping Katy along the road, JT spat in the direction of a fat crow that stood blinking at them just outside the fence. The birds emerged from the farm like sated maggots, taking their time now. The youngest and least disfigured took wing, darting and circling about. The slower ones, misshapen and potbellied, ambled and dragged themselves along without evident concern. One bunch came rolling and sliding in a single column like a feathered serpent, covered in bald patches where stalks had rubbed and pulled plumage free. They looked to have fused or grown together like a huddle of sewer rats. JT was almost sorry he would miss the grisly scene when that thing tried to cross a state highway.

From above, the slow exodus would have resembled a sore oozing dark, oily corruption. If the birds had started west, JT and Katy would have gone south or north; they would not set foot in any direction a single crow went.

For all they knew, another sick pit was crying out for them, calling demon-killers on the wing to some new blind and godless place. From the way they loitered or moved aimlessly across the ground, JT suspected otherwise. The birds moved as if dazed by daylight, as uncertain of their plans as Lazarus newly raised from the dead.

Even so, once the scattering began, it continued without stopping. The farm that had grown so long against its dying neighbors was deadest of all, months passing in minutes as its final signs of life hopped and flapped away like black beetles. Their purpose fulfilled, they struck out into a world which had not thought to keep a place for them.

JT, conjuring old songs in his head to keep both feet moving, considered that he and the others in the camper had vanished from the normal flow of existence when the farm tried to claim them. The longer he and Katy walked, waiting for mountains to rise in their western view, the less likely it seemed that anything would change for the better. JT was sure of Katy's trembling fingers gripping him hard enough to hurt, but as the sun crept mercilessly up toward noon, he wondered whether a disappearing act like theirs, however brief, could really be undone.

He hoped they would find out soon.

THE END?

Not if you want to dive into more of Crystal Lake Publishing's Tales from the Darkest Depths!

Check out our amazing website and online store or download our latest catalog here: https://geni.us/CLPCatalog.

We always have great new projects and content on the website to dive into, as well as a newsletter, behind the scenes options, social media platforms, our own dark fiction shared-world series and our very own webstore. Our webstore even has categories specifically for KU books, non-fiction, anthologies, and of course more novels and novellas.

THE END!

AUTHOR BIOGRAPHIES

Dan Fields absconded with a film degree from Northwestern University. He keeps it in gently scuffed condition and brandishes it on select holidays. He has published fiction with Pseudopod, Nocturnal Transmissions, Hellbound Books, Improbable Press and many more. Between scribbling fits he records and performs with the band Polecat Rodeo in his hometown of Houston, Texas USA. Dan and co-author Chris Robinson (as "Lyman Graves") have published stories with Nocturnal Transmissions, Grotesque Quarterly, The Great Void, and Swamp Ape Review.

See more at danfieldswrites.com.

Chris Robinson is a Houston native with a penchant for wordplay, dogs, and undiscovered monsters. His work has been featured on his mom's refrigerator for decades. Although he has not yet slaughtered the last of the sacred cows, he's deftly managed to milk it.

Joe Filipas studied film and frequently collaborated with Dan Fields at Northwestern University. He was a producer and first Assistant Director on the Student Emmy-winning short *The Detention Teacher*. His short films, including horror shorts *The Garage* and *Bad Habit*, and musical comedy series *Valley Meadows,* have been featured and awarded at LA Webfest, The Minneapolis International Film Festival, The South Dakota Film Festival, and Minneapolis Comic Con. He also has several unfinished manuscripts sitting on his desk in Minneapolis, Minnesota, where he lives with his wife and daughter.

Readers…

Thank you for reading *Harvest Time*. We hope you enjoyed this novel. If you have a moment, please review *Harvest Time* at the store where you bought it.

Help other readers by telling them why you enjoyed this book. No need to write an in-depth discussion. Even a single sentence will be greatly appreciated. Reviews go a long way to helping a book sell, and is great for an author's career. It'll also help us to continue publishing quality books.

Thank you again for taking the time to journey with Crystal Lake's Torrid Waters.

You will find links to all our social media platforms on our Linktree page: https://linktr.ee/CrystalLakePublishing.

MISSION STATEMENT

Since its founding in August 2012, Crystal Lake Publishing has quickly become one of the world's leading publishers of Dark Fiction and Horror books. In 2023, Crystal Lake Publishing formed a part of Crystal Lake Entertainment, joining several other divisions, including Torrid Waters, Crystal Lake Comics, and many more.

While we strive to present only the highest quality fiction and entertainment, we also endeavour to support authors along their writing journey. We offer our time and experience in non-fiction projects, as well as author mentoring and services, at competitive prices.

With several Bram Stoker Award wins and many other wins and nominations (including the HWA's Specialty Press Award), Crystal Lake puts integrity, honor, and respect at the forefront of our publishing operations.

We strive for each book and outreach program we spearhead to not only entertain and touch or comment on issues that affect our readers, but also to strengthen and support the Dark Fiction field and its authors.

Not only do we find and publish authors we believe are destined for greatness, but we strive to work with men and women who endeavour to be decent human beings who care more for others than themselves, while still being hard-working, driven, and passionate artists and storytellers.

Crystal Lake is and will always be a beacon of what passion and dedication, combined with overwhelming teamwork and respect, can accomplish. We endeavour to know each and every one of our readers, while building personal relationships with our authors, reviewers, bloggers, podcasters, bookstores, and libraries.

This is what we believe in. What we stand for. This will be our legacy.

Welcome to Crystal Lake Entertainment.

Also from Torrid Waters...

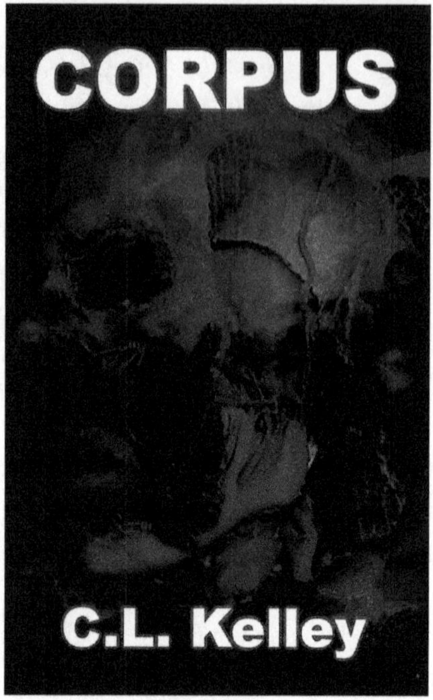

In C.L. Kelley's debut novel Corpus, the city's night transforms into a realm of terror.

Nameless, powerful beings, lost in their hunger and forgotten pasts, roam the streets after sunset. But an awakening stirs within them, sharpening their minds and unearthing memories of a dark history and an even darker future.

This chilling foray into vampire fiction pits the hunter against the hunted in a world brimming with supernatural horror and action. Kelley masterfully intertwines multiple perspectives, each character endowed with unique psychic abilities. At the heart of this narrative is a complex villain protagonist, blurring the lines between hero and villain.

The plot thickens with the presence of shapeshifters, adding layers of unpredictability to the already tense atmosphere. Even the seasoned monster hunters find themselves outmatched by these evolving adversaries. The once comforting break of dawn no longer signifies safety.

C.L. Kelley's Corpus is a thrilling exploration of a world where night creatures are not just real but are becoming something more formidable. It's a tale of survival, where the emergence of the dawn might not end the nightmare.

This novel promises an immersive experience into a spine-tingling universe, where every turn of the page brings you closer to the heart of darkness.

Also from Torrid Waters...

A fast-paced story of survival, terror, family, and friendship.

The people of Wicker thought the mountain belonged to them—purchased with blood, sweat, and resilience. They forgot the deal their ancestors made. They forgot that their mountain belonged to something ancient, powerful, and hungry.

Charlotte Crowe and Rebecca Greenleigh grew up as best friends on the mountain, descendants of the original settlers of Wicker and inheritors of a terrible secret. They expected to grow old on their mountain. They did not expect the return of the wolves, the bone chimes appearing overnight in the trees, or their neighbors turning on one another. In a matter of days, everything they thought they knew is flipped upside down and they find themselves trapped in a place they once called home playing a dangerous game with a creature older than the mountain itself.

THANK YOU FOR PURCHASING THIS BOOK

www.ingramcontent.com/pod-product-compliance
Lightning Source LLC
Chambersburg PA
CBHW070418310726
48977CB00003B/735